Hugh Moises

A Treatise on the Blood

General arrangement of many important facts, relative to the vital fluid : with some

cursory observations on the theory of animal heat - Vol. 2

Hugh Moises

A Treatise on the Blood
General arrangement of many important facts, relative to the vital fluid : with some cursory observations on the theory of animal heat - Vol. 2

ISBN/EAN: 9783337392871

Printed in Europe, USA, Canada, Australia, Japan

Cover: Foto ©Andreas Hilbeck / pixelio.de

More available books at **www.hansebooks.com**

OR, GENERAL ARRANGEMENT OF

MANY

IMPORTANT FACTS,

RELATIVE TO THE

VITAL FLUID.

WITH

SOME CURSORY OBSERVATIONS

ON THE

THEORY OF ANIMAL HEAT.

INTERSPERSED WITH

PATHOLOGICAL and PHYSIOLOGICAL REMARKS

FROM THE

INDUCTIONS of MODERN CHEMISTRY.

Tandem immortalis Harveus difpulfis antiquæ medecinæ tenebris ingens lumen attulit anatomicis imprimis ac Phyfiologicis rebus dum per experimenta in vivis animalibus inftituta detegerct ac publicis fcriptis demonftraret fanguinis circulationem.

Ph. Ambros Marherr.

By HUGH MOISES,

SURGEON OF THE WESTERN REGIMENT OF MIDDLESEX MILITIA, AND LATE SENIOR PUPIL TO THE GENERAL HOSPITAL NOTTINGHAM.

LONDON:

PRINTED FOR T. EVANS, PATERNOSTER ROW, AND J. STEAD, AT THE NAVAL AND MILITARY PRINTING-OFFICE, GOSPORT

Rev. HUGH MOISES,

NEWCASTLE upon TYNE.

P. S. D.

I Should indeed be unworthy of the kind attention you have ever beſtowed on me as your nephew, could I forget the gratitude I owe you ; and not avail myſelf of the opportunity now offered of acknowledging the numerous obligations I lay under to you from your ever anxious ſolicitude in regard to my welfare.

It

It muſt ever be pleaſing to a grateful heart, to ſpeak of the good offices of a friend; but more eſpecially when the connection we have with that friend is ſtrengthened by the ties of conſangui- nity: how much more exhilirating then muſt be that pleaſure, when not only all theſe circumſtances coaleſce, but even to that friend are owing the advantages that have accrued to me in the cultiva- tion of the moſt enlightened and benig- nant of ſciences.

To make uſe of compliment I am well perſuaded would be equally unworthy of yourſelf and me.

Suffice it then to obſerve that the only motives I could entertain in this dedi- cation, are to pay, through the medium of this eſſay, the tribute of gratitude due

to

to your benificence, and to affure you
that an anxious thirft after the knowledge of facts, and for the advancement
of fcience, could alone induce me to enter on the world in fo queftionable a
fhape.

That this laudable intention may in
fome meafure be fulfilled ; and that this
may not altogether prove an *Acharifton*
is the moft ardent wifh of

Your devoted,

Humble Servant,

HUGH MOISES.

ERRATA.

The reader is requested to correct such other errors as the author is sensible must exist; from the hasty manner in which the work has been printed.

PREFACE.

MAN has implanted in his mind a keen defire of knowing whatever can be difcovered, either refpecting himfelf, or the objects which furround him. But the too great eagernefs and impatience with which we almoft univerfally attempt the acquifion of this knowledge, too often leads to hafty and erroneous conclufions.

Time feems as it were to fanction this general diffufion of error, and from cuftom alone it has become venerable; infomuch that fhould we have courage enough to attempt its detection, it is probable we may be branded with the epithet of madnefs or profanity.

" Error,

" Error, fays a very ingenious and truly enlightened author*, triumphs in the fmiles and
countenance of the great, it is diftinguifhed by
titles and rank, and enjoys the folid fupport of
emolument ; and truth, which had all along been
the pretended object of purfuit, is firft thruft down
to the bottom of the pit, and then buried deeper
and deeper under the fucceffive ftrata of falfe
knowledge. Genius is difgraced, difcovery af-
faffinated, and dulnefs eftablifhed in all the pride
of eminent ftation."

Caufes have been affigned before a fufficient
number of facts have been collected, and attempts have been made to reafon from phenomena
not fufficiently underftood, to others equally unknown; thus, inftead of obferving and ftudying
phenomena laborioufly, and patiently collecting
facts, and gradually tracing thefe to more general facts, till at length they arrive at one which

* Vide Brown on Phyfic.

ferves

ferves for a common connecting caufe, the order
of nature in philofophizing is inverted, and the
more general practice has been to begin with the
affumption of a fancied caufe, and afterwards tor-
turing facts into an agreement therewith.

The found philofopher begins with laying in
his ftock of facts. With thefe, by repeated and accurate obfervation he acquires a familiarity, guards
againft the deception of appearances, ftudies and
contemplates the fubject in all its various forms,
and modifications, traces every relation, and
marks every difference, till at laft, by a folid,
cautious, and broad induction, he afcends to a
fact which unites them all, and which itfelf receives illuftration and confirmation from each of
them. For, when any one thing in nature is fully underftood, it leads to the difcovery of fome-
thing next and moft intimately connected with it.
From this the philofopher is led to a fimilar confideration of a third, proceeding as it were from
link to link in one common chain, till he reaches
the

the higheſt ; or he goes on, as it were, from the
ſeveral points in the circumference of a circle
where the radii terminate, along each radius, till
he arrives at the point in which they all meet, conſtituting the centre.

This ultimate fact, at which he at length arrives,
is his common cauſe, the fundamental propoſition
to or from which all his reaſonings flow, and the
baſis on which the whole ſuperſtructure of his doctrine reſts. Still however, he regards this as a fact
only univerſal indeed with reſpect to his ſubject,
but ſubordinate to other facts in the great chain of
which it is only a link, and which according as
they ſtand higher or lower in the ſeries, act as
cauſe or effect on each other.

Finding that this fact connects all the reſt, and
explains all the phenomena, he admits it as the
only cauſe which a philoſopher ought to regard.
Far from bewildering himſelf in vain and fruit-
leſs ſpeculations with reſpect to the nature of
this

this common caufe, confidered abftractly, and as it were, in itfelf in its mode of acting, and fo forth, his great care and attention is to afcertain its exiftence, and get a full and complete acquaintance with the mutual and permanent relations which fubfift between it and the effects.

Thus far he treads on known and firm ground. Here he ftops, and keeps himfelf on fure ground againft the wanderings of fanciful explanation.

The pure ftudy of nature is always fimple, clear, and fatisfactory, while on the contrary every diviation from it, leads but to a wildernefs of error and inextricable perplexity. The light arifing from the former, and the darknefs from the latter, are in exact proportion to the refpective progrefs of each.

The ftudent of nature moves at firft with caution, flownefs, and circumfpection ; proceeding afterwards with freedom, firmnefs, and eafe, in

pro-

proportion to the illumination encreaſing around him. And has been compaŕed to a traveller, beginning his journey with the earlieſt dawn of day*.

The flights of an heated imagination unreſtrained by reflection, and a ſtrict regard to fact, may produce an evaneſcent temporary gratification ; but the diſcovery of truth alone, can yield that moſt pure and exquiſite ſatisfaction, that ſolid and permanent pleaſure, which muſt ever ſucceed, to ſucceſs, in any important philoſophical inveſtigation.

The former is the ravings and intoxication of miſguided ſpeculation, but the latter only can afford a rational and ſound delight.

The former is but a ſhadowy, unſubſtantial joy, a mental titillation, a paroxyſm of exultation which muſt unavoidably be ſucceded by diſmay

* Vide Brown on Phyſic.

and

and regret, on the firſt diſcovery of its deluſive cauſe.

How widely, different from this, the pleaſure afforded to Pythogoras on his diſcovery of the 47th problem of the firſt book of Euclid ; or that of Lord Naper upon his diſcovery of the lo-garithms ; or the ſerene and ſolid ſatisfaction of mind which Sir Iſaac Newton experienced on finding his fundamental principle apply to the whole phenomena of his great and extenſive ſub-ject, producing a ſcientific body of knowledge, which a learned author before quoted, calls " The " ſcience of the motion of all the great bodies in " the ſolar ſyſtem, and probably in all the ſyſ- " tems of the univerſe." Illuſtrious name ! Irre-fragable proof of man's vaſt genius, and the ſoar-ing ſoul !

The great buſineſs of a true philoſopher, is to encreaſe the number, and improve the knowledge of uſeful and important facts, and at the ſame

time

time to render them ftill more beneficial and fub-
fervient to human happinefs, while the falfe philofopher, deeming this employment below his attention, or difcouraged with a labour too tedious
and arduous for his ftock of patience and induf-
try, as perhaps wholly ignorant of the only proper
method of profecuting philofophical enquiry,
rufhes onward to the ultimate end of his object,
little ftudious of the beft means of attaining it.

Inftead therefore, of labouring by obfervation
and experiment, to enlarge the number of folid
and ufeful facts, from which alone, by juft and
careful induction, the laws of nature in any of
her departments can be afcertained; his vain attempt is to difcover the abftract nature, the mode
of operation, the hidden caufe of the fact, which
his author had taken for his common connecting
caufe, and which from the limited nature of the
human faculties he had been obliged to confider
as an ultimate fact, or as a law of nature, of which

no

no caufe more general than itfelf could be affigned.

Finding, therefore in the great chain of caufe
and effect, nothing more general, and impelled
by an avidity inherent in the human mind, of
preffing forward to the attainment of knowledge
beyond its power, he at once plunges himfelf into
an ocean of endlefs hypothefis, and thereby brings
reproach, in the very principles on which he refts
it, on the doctrine or branch of knowledge, which
it was his intention to improve.

Before the method of philofophizing by induction was known, the hypothefes of philofophers
were wild, fanciful, and ridiculous. They had
recourfe to æther, occult qualities, and other imaginary caufes, in order to explain the various phenomena of nature : but fince the time of the
great Lord Verulam, who may be deemed the
parent of genuine philofophy, a contrary courfe
has happily been followed.

b

He

He convinced the world, that all knowledge muſt be derived from experiment and obſervation; and that every attempt to inveſtigate cauſes by any other means muſt eventually prove unſuccefsful. Since his time, the beſt philoſophers have followed the path which he pointed out. Boyle, Locke, Newton, Hales, and a few others, in little more than one century, improved and extended ſcience far beyond what the accumulated force of all the preceding philoſophers, even perhaps from the creation, had been able to effectuate.

Dean Swift ſeems to explain in the moſt ſatisfactory manner, that propenſity in the human mind which prompts us to attempt the ſolution of things eventually beyond our reach.

" Let us examine ſays he, the great introducers
" of new ſchemes in philoſophy, and ſearch till we
" can find from what faculty of the ſoul the dif-
" poſition ariſes in mortal man, of taking it into
" his

" his head to advance new systems, with such an
" eager zeal, in things agreed on all hands *impossi-*
" *ble* to be known ; from what seeds this dispo-
" sition springs, and to what quality of human
" nature these grand innovators have been in-
" debted for their number of disciples ; because
" it is plain, that several of the chief among them,
" both *ancient* and *modern* were usually mistaken by
" their adversaries, and indeed by all except their
" own followers, to have been persons crazed, or
" out of their wits ; having generally proceeded
" in the common course of their words and acti-
" ons, by a method very different from the vul-
" gar dictates of unrefined reason, agreeing for
" the most part, in their several models, with their
" present undoubted successors in the *academy of*
" *modern bedlam.* Of this kind were *Epicurus, Di-*
" *ogenes, Apollonius, Lucretius, Paracelsus, De Cartes*
" and others ; who, if they were now in this
" world, tied fast, and separated from their fol-
" lowers would, in this *undistinguishing* age, incur
" manifest danger of *phlebotomy,* and *whips,* and
                                            chains

" *chains*, and *dark chambers*, and *ſtraw*. For what
" man, in the natural ſtate or courſe of thinking,
" did ever conceive it in his power to reduce the
" notions of all makind exactly to the ſame breadth,
" and length, with his own ? Yet this is the firſt
" *humble* and *civil* deſign in all innovations in the
" empire of reaſon. Now, I would gladly be in-
" formed, how it is poſſible to account for ſuch
" imaginations as theſe in particular men, with-
" out recourſe to my *phenomena* of vapours (i. e.
" æther) aſcending from the lower faculties to
" overſhadow the brain, and there diſtilling into
" conception, for which the narrowneſs of our mo-
" ther-tongue has not yet aſſigned any other name
" beſides that of *madneſs* or *phrenzy*. Let us there-
" fore now conjecture how it comes to paſs that
" none of theſe great projectors do ever fail pro-
" viding themſelves and their notions with a
" number of *implicit diſciples* ; and I think the rea-
" ſon is eaſy to be aſſigned.—For there is a pecu-
" liar ſtring in the harmony of human under-
" ſtanding, which in ſeveral individuals, is exactly

" of

" of the fame tuning. This if you can dextroufly
" *fcrew* up to its right key, and then *ftrike gently*
" upon it, whenever you have the good fortune to
" light among thofe of the *fame pitch*, they will,
" by a fecret neceffary fympathy, ftrike exactly at
" the fame time. And in this one circumftance
" lies all the *skill* or *luck* of the matter : for if
" you chance to jar the ftring, among thofe who
" are either above or below your own height, in-
" ftead of fubfcribing to your doctrine, they will
" *tie you faft,* call you *mad,* and feed you with
" *bread* and *water.* It is therefore a point of the
" niceft conduct, to diftinguifh and adapt this
" noble talent with refpect to the difference of
" *perfons* and of *times.*—For, to fpeak a bold truth,
" it is a fatal mifcarriage fo ill to order affairs as
" to pafs for a *fool* in one company, while in
" another you might be treated as a *philofo-*
" *pher.*"

From what we have already obferved, it would
feem to be obvioufly inferred, that an accurate
know-

knowledge of the phenomena is the only bafis on which convictive reafonings, fatisfactory explanations, and found theories can be eftablifhed. Analogical arguments prefent themfelves readily to a warm imagination, whilft thofe more decifive ones arifing from experiment, can only be obtained by labour and painful attention. Hence even in the moft important fubjects the former are fubftituted in place of the latter, and after the moft beautiful fyftem has been formed, fome paltry little fact is difcovered, which overthrows the whole, and turns its fabricator into ridicule. If analogy, next to experiment, be in philofophical inveftigation the fureft guide, it muft always influence the judgement in proportion to the ftrength of the refemblance, and the number of circumftances in which fimilarity is found. Hence, it is not without reafon that we are backward in believing what appears to us contrary to the general phenomena of nature ; but it is the duty of every lover of truth not to fuffer himfelf to be fo much actuated by that ftrong propenfity, which

in

induces us to refer all knowledge to certain principles, as to fuppofe the laws of nature fewer and
more fimple than they really are. From this im-
patient defire of generalizing has fprung the too
hafty reduction of fcience into fyftem, which
is perhaps one of the chief caufes that have re-
tarded the advancement of natural knowledge ;
for though on a fuperficial furvey of the works of
nature, fhe may feem to have uniformly operated
on the fame plan, yet when we contemplate her
with more attention and inveftigate with more accuracy the mode and fyftem of her operations, we
are then no lefs aftonifhed at the variety of the de-
fign, than at the multiplicity of the means of ex-
ecution---

    " And every view convincing marks impart,
    "Of perfect wifdom and ftupendous art!

The antients expreffed lefs aftonifhment than
we do at the facts which they could not explain.

They were convinced, that man can only perceive a few of the moft obvious fprings employed
                             by

by nature in the execution of her various defigns, and therefore pronounced it prefumptuous in him to think of limiting her to a definite number of principles of action. But thefe fages carried their circumfpection and diffidence to an improper length, for by thus difcouraging an active fpirit of enquiry they effectually checked the progrefs of natural fcience. It is of the utmoft importance in philofophy to afcertain, as accurately as poffible the more general powers in nature, and to deter- mine their caufes, and trace their confequences ; for as the phenomena of nature are infinite, and the faculties of the human mind, particularly the memory, limited, when thefe phenomena are con- fidered as unconnected with other facts, they con- vey but little inftruction. The infinite is not the object of fcience, and therefore till the laws of nature are known, by a careful obfervation of in- dividuals, and an accurate induction from them, no progrefs can be made in natural philofophy. Hence the neceffity of collecting and connecting correfponding facts, and the advantage of reducing

them

them to certain general principles, and of applying thefe to account for other phenomena; for
thus by a flow and cautious induction we may advance to a knowledge of the moft general laws
that regulate the fyftem of nature. But though
we be warranted to confider all the phenomena
that we find connected with thefe general laws,
and manifeftly depending upon them as fo many
facts explained, fo many truths known and underftood, yet we ought not to overlook fuch phenomena, as are not reducible to thefe general principles, but fhould view them as fimple and feparate facts, and treafure them up till a more en-
larged experience, and more accurate obfervation
lead us to the difcovery of the powers of nature,
to which they fhould be referred.

In the courfe of the following fheets we have
uniformly endeavoured to adhere as clofely as
poffible to thefe principles, and the matter though
arranged in a fcattered and defultory manner is,
we truft, pregnant with many important facts,

c   each

each deriving their origin from a different author without ever having been collected into one
general point of view.

A confiderable part of the materials which have
compofed this work, were originally collected as
notes, in my perufal of different authors, without the moft diftant idea of publication; but finding them encreafe very confiderably both as to
number and importance, I attempted their arrangement in as accurate and connected a manner
as the numerous avocations of public practice
would allow; how far I have fucceeded does not
become me to judge;---with diffidence I fubmit
them to the public, and requefting only that portion of indulgence which is ever due to a laudable
inclination.

I am not unaware of the difficulties which perhaps every young author muft encounter, efpecially in a firft publication, and which are fufficient to damp the ardour even of the moft active
genius.

Cri-

Criticifm, as the bird of prey, lays wait efpecially for the difcovery of error in the *young* ; fatire
prepares its keeneft fhafts ; the merits of the
work, if it has any fuch, are not unfrequently o-
verlooked, and its defects as feduloufly held forth
to the eyes of the world.

Such is too frequently the fate of a firft production, unlefs it is brought forward to public
notice, by the recommendatory influence of fome
great authority, or fupported by a fanction which
may command refpect. I am confcious that many
imperfections will be found to exift in the arrangement of the fubject matter of this work, and no
lefs fenfible, that, in all probability it contains a
too plentiful harveft of errors, which may no
doubt afford ample fcope for *puny* criticifm ;
whilft I chear myfelf with the hope, that the liberal critic, and the *ftudent* in medical philofophy,
will find feveral difficulties cleared up, and many
important facts taken notice of, which were before
wanting, or not generally underftood, and which
may not prove altogether unacceptable.

Should

Should the public favour me with their approbation, and not frown upon my undertaking ; inftead of repining at the want of fome compendious fyftem of medical knowledge, I fhall endeavour to remedy it, to the beft of fuch abilities as I poffefs, by prefenting it with a fyftem of medical fcience compiled from the works of the moft eminent and approved authors, which, though it may not have to boaft of much originality, fhall at leaft evince the candour of a genuine eclectic. In the mean time, my requeft from the learned of time, and the ripened of ages, is this,---" Wherever there fhall occur an omiffion or error, cover it with the mantle of generofity, and hold the pen of correction running over it. "

A TREA-

A

TREATISE on the BLOOD.

By the blood, fome have underftood not only the fluids in the veins and arteries, but likewife that in the lymphatics, nerves, and every other veffel of the body, becaufe they fuppofed all their contents to be parts of the blood feparated from it, by the force of the heart; and many of them return to it again after the performance of their deftined office. And in this acceptation it has been taken in the calculations of its quantities and velocities, in the human body. But thefe muft be very erroneous, fince they will always vary in degrees, according to the different temperaments, fexes and ages, and the different quantities of action in each.

Hence

Hence it appears a difficult matter to determine with any degree of accuracy what proportion the fluids of an animal body, bear to the folids ; or what proportion the fum of all the moft minute arteries bear to the aorta ; without which I fhould think we can neither determine the comparative velocity of the blood moving in the different vef-fels, nor the quantity of blood in any animal body, nor the time in which the whole mafs of blood, or a quantity equal to the whole mafs, is flowing through the heart. Yet as it is often requifite to draw blood in the practice of medicine and again to repeat it, it has been fuppofed neceffary to know the quantity of blood contained in an animal body, in order to proportion the quantity, at any time to be taken away, to the fize and other par-ticular circumftances of the patient.

Various methods have been taken by different Phyfiologifts to afcertain this : as the weighing an animal, and bleeding it to death, then fubtracting the weight of the blood from that of the whole
animal

animal. Dr. Haller bled a horfe to the quantity of twenty eight pounds before he died; and another of much the fame fize loft forty four pounds before he was exhaufted. Hence it is obvious this method muft be very fallacious and uncertain, as the animal dies long before all the blood is drawn away; for on examining the body afterwards, we always find a quantity of blood in *fome* of the veffels.

Others have endeavoured to determine this point by collecting and comparing different cafes of hæmorrhagy. We have an inftance of a perfon lofing twenty-nine pounds of blood in twenty-four hours by vomiting---Sanctorious mentions an inftance of a man lofing forty pounds of blood in four days by a nafal hæmorrhage, and another Author relates the cafe of one who loft feventy-five pounds of blood in ten days by the piles.

The exhauftion depends more on the ftate of the

veffels and the manner in which the blood is difcharged, than on the quantity---for one pound of
blood loft in five minutes will exhauft an animal
more, than two pounds taken away in two hours,
as in proportion to the rapidity with which the
blood flows the animal will be ,fooner or later exhaufted : for it muft be obvious to every one that
(cæteris paribus) the evacuation of blood from a
large veffel near the heart will deftroy a perfon
fooner, than when coming from a fmall veffel at a
greater diftance from the heart.—The momentum
and velocity of the blood being proportionably
more confiderable in the larger veffels.

If the ventricles of the heart hold five ounces of
blood, and they are filled and emptied every fyftole
and diaftole ; of which there are many cogent
proofs : and if eighty pulfes in a minute be allowed
to be a common number, there then flows twenty-
five pounds of blood through each ventricle of the
heart in a minute. Dr. Keil has fhewn that the
fum of all the fluids, exceed that of the folids,
and

and yet the quantity of blood which all the *vifible* arteries of a man will contain, does not exceed four pounds ; and if we may fuppofe all the veins, including the fyftem of the vena portæ, held four times as much*, the whole then that the viffible veffels *can* contain is not more than twenty pounds, but the whole that they *do* contain, is very little more than the veins themfelves are capable of containing, as is evident from the arteries being always found nearly empty in dead bodies.

But how much the arteries and veins contain† I know of no means whereby to form a decifive judgement ; unlefs we know what proportions thefe veffels bear to thofe which carry the nutritious juices and ferum without the red globules of

---

* Haller has come nearer the truth in this proportion, by allowing four parts to the arteries, and nine to the veins.

† I mean thofe which carry a compound fluid, fuch as is found in the larger veffels.

the

the blood. Cæteris paribus, is not the velocity of the blood and the neceſſity of taking food in all animals, proportionable to their quantities of action? If ſo, we may readily underſtand how thoſe animals which uſe no exerciſe and whoſe blood moves extremely ſlow in the winter, can ſubſiſt without any freſh ſupply of food, while others, which uſe a little more exerciſe, require a proportionably greater quantity of nutritious aliment; and thoſe again, which uſe equal exerciſe winter and ſummer, require equal quantities of food in both ſeaſons. The purpoſe of eating and drinking being to repair what exerciſe and the motion of the blood has deſtroyed or rendered uſeleſs. And, is not the leſs velocity of the blood in ſome animals than in others the reaſon why wounds and bruiſes in thoſe animals do not ſo ſoon deſtroy life as they do in animals whoſe blood moves ſwifter?

The ſpecific gravity of the blood, according to the experiments of Mr. Boyle, is, as 1041 to 1000; but, according to thoſe of Dr. Javrin, as 1054 to 1000,

1000, as related by him in the Philofophical Tranfactions. Both Mr. Boyle's and Dr. Javrin's experiments might be accurate, though they differ ; as
its fpecific gravity varies in different, or even in
the fame, amimals at different times, according to
the proportion of its component parts, which have
different fpecific gravities varying from each o-
ther, as the red globules are heavier than either
the gelatinous lymph or ferum, in proportion to
the quantity of ferruginous matter they contain.

The blood is the moft important and the moft
impenetrable of the recrementitious humours : it is
the fource, and, as it were, the focus of all the o-
ther animal fluids. Though many of them are
not to be found originally in the blood, they having undergone very confiderable alterations in the
courfe of their fecretion, according to the fpecific
action of their peculiar fecretory organs. Perhaps fome combinations of which we are unac-
quainted, take place in thefe veffels. Many Phyficians, and more particularly Mr. Bordeu, confidered

fidered it as a kind of fluid flesh, and as a compound of all the other animal humours ; and though this opinion has not been proved by any well attested facts, yet it is by some suppofed to be highly probable.

Though we have hitherto failed in demonftrating the exiftence of many of thofe fecretions *un-combined* in the mafs of blood ; yet we are not rafhly to infer that thefe can claim no origin from it, becaufe experiments have not hitherto fucceeded in feparating them wholly from their different combinations. The operations of nature are in many inftances very obfcure, and though our predeceffors have not hitherto been fo fortunate as to refolve the myftery, yet fhe may be more indulgent to fome future favourite. We may naturally fuppofe fhe would not exhauft her enigmatic ftore on the prefent race, to the prejudice of our fucceffors, and thereby plunge fucceffive generations into a ftate of inactivity and indolence. No, the capricious dame favours not fuch

fatal

fatal partiality; on the contrary, we find the refolution of almoft every problem, leads but to
others, perhaps ftill more obfcure.

The blood differs very confiderably, according
to the vifcera which contain it, and the regions
through which it paffes; it is not, for inftance,
the fame in the arteries and in the veins, in the ftomach and in the region of the liver, in the fpleen
and in the kidneys; in the mufcles and in the
glands, &c.

When we confider the blood with refpect to the
whole animal kingdom, we may obferve that it
varies very remarkably in different animals, and
in the different fpecies of the fame animal; and
even, as I have before obferved, in the fame individual at different times, with regard to colour,
fmell, confiftence, and more efpecially temperature. This laft property is the moft important, and
appears from many well grounded arguments to
depend conjointly on refpiration and circulation.

B   The

The blood of man, quadrupeds, and birds, is hotter than the medium they inhabit, being more than the mean degree of atmofpheric heat, but lefs than the greateft—they are therefore called animals with warm blood—In fifhes and reptiles it comes pretty near the temperature of the medium they inhabit; from which they are called animals with cold blood. It is probable that differences equally confiderable would be found to obtain in all the other properties of this fluid, and more efpecially in its chemical qualities and characters, if the blood of all animals were properly examined. Dr. Wrisberg, of Gottingen, fays that daily experience evinces that the blood of man to which our attention is more particularly directed, varies according to age, fex, temperament, ftate of health of the individual, motion or reft of body, ftate of mind, climate, kind of life, weather, meat and drink, and the various fpecies and violence of difeafes*.

* See Profeffor Wrifberg's edition of Haller's Phyfiology.

In

In infancy, in the female fex, and in confum¡ tive perfons it is more pale and thin; in robu.. and healthy men, it is thicker, of a deeper colour, inclining to black, and of a much more faline tafte, than in fuch as are weak, and feed on aliments which afford but very little nourifhment, and in whom it is generally of a yellowifh colour.

That its degree of heat may be fomewhat augmented by an increafe of heat in the atmofphere, is moft certain ; but it does not rife to the greateft pitch of fummer heat. We can live in a much greater heat than that of the warmeft fummer, as is proved by perfons employed in fugar houfes, melting furnaces, by mowers, and the ufe of ftoves in Finland and in Ruffia ; as alfo by fome late experiments of Fordyce, Blagden, Hunter and Dobfon. The natural heat of the blood is fometimes fo di.. minifhed in an intenfe cold, that in a perfon froft. bitten, but not dead, Fahrenheit's thermometer would not rife above 76°, though applied to the armpits, mouth, groins, and even the vagina.

That

That the matter of heat is inherent in the blood alone, and thereby transfufed over the fyftem; is rendered fufficiently probable from different phenomena; for the heat of the body is diminifhed by hæmorrhagy in proportion to the quantity of blood loft, or when the flow of blood is intercepted by ligature or compreffion from reaching the joints, and the heat returns when the parts are reftored to their natural ftate. This would feem to be confirmed by a very general obfervation that when the powers of life are brought very low, and vigour is wanted to carry on the ufual functions, - . the fanguiferous fyftem becomes affected in the moft fenfible manner, and its action being no longer able to propel the blood to thofe parts of the machine which are moft diftant from the heart, their temperature begins to decreafe, and continues to diminifh in proportion as the circulation declines. Hence it is ufual to judge of the approach of death by the coldnefs of the extremities; for notwithftanding one or two feeming exceptions, it is an incontrovertible truth, that ani-

mated

mated bodies lofe heat in a given temperature
of air, as faft as any unorganized matter, of the
fame bulk, of a texture any way fimilar, and
heated to the fame degree. In fhort fo very numerous and ftriking are the facts which evince the
connection between the ftate of motion of the fanguiferous fyftem, and the temperature of the body,
that no doubt can be juftly entertained of the latter being in a fecondary manner, at leaft, the effect of the former; for no fooner has the circulation taken place, than the temperature falls or
rifes, according as the motion of the blood is encreafed or diminifhed. Of this we have given the
cleareft evidence in the cafe of dying perfons.

It was the opinion of the late learned Lord
Bacon, that no vegetable, any more than the moft
inorganic matter, is poffeffed of a degree of heat
beyond that of the furrounding medium, and he
expreffes himfelf to this effect in the following
terms " In vegetabilibus et plantis mullus repe-
" ritur caloris gradus neque in lachrymis ipfo-
" rum

"rum, neque in medullis recenter apertis." But, by the experiments of Mr. John Hunter, it would appear that *living plants* have a power of refifting, for a certain time, the communication of cold, or at leaft that they are longer in freezing than *dead* vegetables*. If this be really the cafe, as I doubt not it is, Lord Bacon's opinion muft fall to the ground, and, confequently, all conclu-fions deduced therefrom.

One of the moft remarkable phenomena of *animal heat* is the uniformity which it is obferved to maintain under the greateft irregularity of fize, infomuch that we cannot perceive any difference to take place from age, fex, fize, or temperament. Dr. Hean (in his Ralio Medendi) has rendered this fufficiently clear with refpect to man, by a courfe of accurate experiments on fubjects of both fexes, from the earlieft infancy, to extreme old age : and, if we may be allowed to reafon from

* Vide Philofophical Tranfactions, Vol. 65.

ana-

analogy, we may fuppofe that the fame uniformity of temperature extends to all the more perfect tribes of animals. Before the time of the im-
mortal *Harvey*, Phyfiologifts were of opinion that
the fpecific heat of fome parts of the body, was
greater than that of others, but *Malphighi*, in his
pofthumous works, affirms that it is uniformly the
fame throughout the whole body. That it is
always fo, cannot poffibly be admitted by any one
who is at all acquainted with the phenomena of
inflammation ; and that it is in *general* the cafe
feems very dubious, from the following experiment, which was inftituted in order to afcertain
the different degrees of heat between arterial and
venous blood. Having procured two dogs of the
fame age and temperature, I divided the carotid
artery of one and immediately applied a thermometer of very extenfive range to the ftream, the
mercury rofe to 97° ¼ and in the courfe of ten
feconds fell to 96° ¼—I then divided the jugular
vein of the other, and in like manner applied the
thermometer to the ftream, but the mercury only

rofe

rofe to *fomewhat* above 96°—In this experiment
I could not help remarking the different quantities
of time required, for the coagulation of the blood.
The *arterial blood*, though in much the fame
quantity and ftanding in the fame place and temperature with the venous, was not perfectly coagulated, till *upwards of three minutes* after the
procefs of coagulation in the *venous* was completed*.

That the *matter of heat* is taken in by refpiration feems evident from the refult of various experiments, as well as from accurate obfervation of
its natural phenomena ; for I have had frequent
opportunities of obferving that in proportion as
refpiration was more or lefs free, fo would be the

---

* It is very probable that a confiderable portion of the
caloric principle of vital air, or *oxyginous gaz* is feparated
from arterial blood, previous to the bloods circulating through
the *veins*.—Hence may arife proportionate variations in their
quantities of *heat*—But of this and other differences we fhall
have occafion to fpeak hereafter.

fpecific

specific heat of the animal, and that both these were intimately connected with the degree of perfection in the state of the animal. That there is an intimate connection between the *colour* and the *heat* of the blood seems evident from what Haller says in his Element. Physiolog. that the blood of fishes, has neither heat nor density, and but very little craffamentum ; in this affertion he is supported by Lewenhoeck's Microfcopical Experiments ; and, I might add to this, that thofe which are deftitute of gills, have their fluids as tranfparent as the element in which they live, and are nearly of the fame temperature ; of this tribe are many of the fpecies of fhell fifh, as oyfters, cockles, &c.

Whilft the circulation of the blood continues vigorous and unimpaired, external circumftances produce little or no change in the temperature of the body ; but as foon as the motion of the heart ceafes, and the blood has begun to ftagnate in its veffels the abfence of the generating caufe of heat

C   becomes

becomes manifeft, and the exanimated mafs now finks to the temperature of the furrounding bodies.

It hath been imagined by many Phyfiologifts that animal heat was produced by mechanical means; in oppofition to which *De Haen** relates, as unanfwerable objections to its mechanical gene-ration, two cafes which fell within his own obfer-vation. In the one he found the temperature of his patient, which during the courfe of an inflam-matory fever had never rifen above 103°, ftood at the time he expired, and for two minutes after at 106°. The heat of the other, who was dying of a lingering diftemper, rofe in the laft agony from 100 to 101° and continued there ftationary for two hours, and even at the expiration of fifteen hours had only fallen to 85° though the furround-ing medium did not exceed 60°.

I perfectly coincide with *De Haen* that thofe

* Ratio Medendi, Vol. 1ft. and 2nd.

caufes

caufes are utterly inexplicable on mechanical principles, and have only to obferve, that the vital
principle is not always extinguifhed immediately
on the ceafing of refpiration as is evident from the
records of the Humane Society, through the happy inftitution of which the vital and natural functions of many have been called into action a confiderable time after *apparent* death.

It was fuppofed by Vanhelmont, Sylvius, and
other chymico phyfiologifts that animal heat
was the refult of *Chymical Mixture* taking place in
fome part of the alimentary canal. Others that
acids, taken into the fyftem, met with alkalies
which in their union generated heat. Thofe however were mere conjectures unfupported by facts :
and did we even admit thefe fuppofitions fo ftated
in their full extent; ftill would they be found in-
fufficient to account for the ftability of animal
heat in different climates and feafons ; its equability all over the body (if fuch equability exift)
when in health ; its partial encreafe in topical in-

flammation ;

flammation ; or fcarcely, indeed, for any one phenomena attending its production.

Putrifactive fermentation has been imagined to
produce heat ; but every argument that can be
adduced in favour of that hypothefis muft at
once be overturned by the confideration of this
obvious fact. That heat is far more confiderable
in a living than in a dead body* ; and no rational
Phyfiologift will deny that the putrid fermentation goes on more rapidly in the latter than in the
former. Others again have fuppofed this principle to be the effect of *mechanical attrition*†, but in
order to refute this it will be fufficient only to remark that the conquaffation of fluids does not
produce heat, but on the contrary makes them

---

* " Si a putredine calor nafcaretur · cadaver calcret poft
mortem, et febri torqueretur ardentius quam dum, viveret,"
Helmont. De Febr. Cap. I.

† See Dr. Martin Edn. Med. Effays, Vol. 3—Dr. Douglas
and many others.

lofe

lofe that which they might previoufly poffefs. And the circulation of the blood through its canals, is ftrictly no more than the action of fluid upon fluid, and no one will aver that fluids are either hard or dry ; two conditions abfolutely neceffary to the mechanical production of heat. Dr. Cullen imagined the different degrees of heat in different animals to be owing to the difference of the vital principle*. But what juft grounds have we to imagine the principle of life different in different animals ? Or how are we to conceive that the fame degree of motion fhould in one clafs of animals always produce a certain degree of heat; and in another clafs as uniformly a different ? Dr. Cullen's hypothefis therefore unfupported by any well attefted facts, muft one day, like thofe of his predeceffors, be configned to oblivion.

Some again have imagined animal heat to be in-herent in the nervous fyftem, but Mr. John Hun-

* Vide Inftitut. Med. p. 224.

ter

ter, feems wholly to have refuted that opinion*.

It has been fuppofed that the fubtle principle,
by chemifts called *phlogifton* which they imagined
to enter into the compofition of every natural
body, was by the action of the vafcular fyftem
gradually evolved through every part of the animal
machine, and that during this evolution heat was
generated‡, but as the exiftence of fuch a principle, cannot by any plaufible facts be eftablifhed,
this theory muft of confequence be thrown afide.
This hypothefis was taught by Dr. Duncan; and
one very fimilar by Dr. Franklin, as alfo by Dr.
Mortimer.†

Gaubins, imagining the red globules to be of an
oily nature, fuppofes them beft calculated for the
generation of animal heat. Haller, on the other

* See Philofophical Tranfactions Vol. 66.

‡ See Leflie on Animal Heat.

† See Philofoph. Tranfact.Vol, 45.

hand,

hand, confiders the iron prefent in the blood as neceffary to the production of heat: however widely thefe two laft authors differ in this matter, yet they agree in afcribing the heat of animals and the colour of their blood to one and the fame caufe; for while Dr. Haller fuppofes both to depend on the quantity of iron contained in the blood. Profeffor Gaubins as confidently imputes them to a quantity of phlogifton (as he calls it) prefent in that fluid, as appears from the follow-ing, and many other paffages in his works. " Rubri fanguinis exceffus cum phlogifton in " fanguine abundans notet, quavis occafione no-" civa, caloris augmenta immodicas expanfiones " inflammationes creat."—Patholog.

It was the opinion of Dr. Black, that, as not only breathing animals, are of all others the warmeft, but alfo as there fubfifts fo clofe a con-nection between the ftate of refpiration and the degree of heat in animals, that they appear to be in an exact proportion to one another; animal

heat

heat depended on refpiration, that it was all generated in the lungs by the action of the air, upon
the principle of inflammability, in a manner little
diffimilar to what occurs in actual inflammation;
and that it is thence diffufed by means of the circulation through the reft of the vital fyftem*.

Of all the various *theories* I have here ftated,
that of Dr. Black feems to come neareft the truth;
and I am inclined to think, that if the laft mentioned author had purfued his enquiry relative to
latent heat, and the generation of carbonic acid,
but a very little further, he would have had the
honour of difcovering firft, what the French chemifts are now beginning to eftablifh.

To many it may, no doubt, appear foreign to
the general tenour of this work, that I fhould
have entered fo fully on this fubject; but, confi-
dering its very great importance in the animal

* See Maclurg Differt. Phyf. de Calore. Edinburg. 1772.

œconomy, and the many obftinate controverfies it
has given rife to*; I thought it a duty incum-
bent on me to fketch out as concifely as I could,
the principal theories, that have at different times
been advanced, for the purpofe of explaining this
curious phenomenon. Thus, the reader will be
left to judge for himfelf, and for a more full explanation of the different hypothefes, he is refered
to the authors above quoted. In the mean time I
fhall attempt, in the fame brief manner, to account for this phenomenon, on the principles
which appear to me beft grounded; and which, I
believe, have already met with the attention of
many enlightened philofophers.

We have already remarked, that animal heat
and refpiration were moft intimately connected;
and it is upon this principle we go, in the deduc-
tion of the following theory.

* The *expence* incurred by the *purchafe* of fo many authors as have written on this fubject, would, no doubt with
many, be a weighty confideration.

D   Atmof-

Atmofpheric air, according to Mr. Lavoifier, is compofed of one part of *carbonic acid*, twenty-feven of vital air, or *oxygenous gaz*, and feventy-two of *azotic gaz*, or atmofpheric mephitis.

The *lungs* are the organs deftined for the important functions of refpiration; and their mechanical ftructure * is moft peculiarly adapted for the purpofe of bringing the blood into contact with the external air, and thereby affording it an opportunity of recovering from the *atmofphere* fuch principles as are neceffary to the welfare of animal life, and which had been feparated from it in the courfe of circulation; as well as to free itfelf of fuch matters, as are either prejudicial, or at leaft not *neceffary* to an healthy ftate in the animal.

*. For a defcription of their mechanifm, we muft refer to anatomical authors, who have defcribed their beautiful and varying ftructure, in a manner equally elegant and accurate. See Monro, Winflow, Haller, Douglas, and many others.

In

In the act of *respiration*, the external air is brought into contact with the *blood* as it passes through the lungs ; and, by a change of principles, or rather by a double affinity, supplys the latter with salutary principles while the atmosphere becomes so vitiated, as to be no longer fit for the purposes of respiration.

In order to explain this, it will be necessary to remark that *oxygenous gaz* is composed of the *caloric* and *oxygenous principles*, and that the blood contains more or less of the carbonaceous principle ; it is with this *carbonaceous principle* that the *oxygene* of the atmosphere unites during the act of respiration, producing *carbonic acid*, which is afterwards, either wholly or in part, carried off along with *azotic gaz* in the succeeding expiration, leaving the *caloric principle* of oxygenous gaz to be diffused through the system, in the course of circulation*.

* The inhalents on the surface of the body no doubt contribute to this effect, though by no means in so considerable a degree.

The

That hydrogene gaz is exhaled from the blood
during refpiration, and, uniting with the oxygene
of the atmofphere forms *water*, feems evident from
the very commonly obferved, though curious fact,
of the breath of animals condenfed on glafs, producing water, which is compofed of the hydro-
genous and oxygenous principles.

Dr. Crawford's experiments and obfervations
on this fubject are truly interefting and ingenious,
though wholly fuperfeded by modern difcoveries*.

From the preceding obfervations it may not
be difficult to account for the deleterious confequences which enfue from confinement in clofe
places, and more efpecially when in confiderable
numbers as in theatres, prifons, hofpitals and in
the holds of fhips, &c. In the latter, Dr. Trotter

---

* See Crawford on Animal Heat. A tract which I fuppofe
to be in the hands of every one; and whofe doctrines therefore it will not be neceffary to infert here.

has

has obferved that they are often ftowed fo clofe, that it is difficult to move without treading upon them. And fpeaking of the apartments in an African flave fhip, he fays, "The temperature in "thefe apartments when they became crowded, "was fometimes above 96° of Farenheit's fcale*." He adds, "I myfelf, could never breathe there, "unlefs under the hatchway. In fuch fituations "it may be fuppofed that the fufferings of thefe "creatures are fometimes dreadful. Air heated "and rarified to fuch a degree, and loaded with "animal effluvia, cannot fail of being noxious "to life ; there were *certainly* inftances where fome "expired from *fuffocation*, having fhewn no pre- "vious figns of indifpofition†. During this feafon "of the year" he adds "there was little rain, and "the weather was not more fultry than is ufual "in thefe latitudes."

* Vide Trotter's obfervations on the fcurvy, Edit. 1792, p. 54.

† Vide Dr. Trotter's evidence on the Slave Trade, before the felect committee of the Houfe of Commons;

That

That thefe effects are not always produced by numbers of individuals collected together and confined in a fmall compafs, feems obvious from the following fact.

Out of upwards of 1600 prifoners, confined in the French prifon at Forton near Gofport, the average number of fick has never exceeded 70 although they are very much crowded during the *night** ; whereas in the Regiment now doing duty there, the average of fick has been upwards of 40 for a confiderable time paft ; while the number of privates in the Regiment (non-effectives†) included) has I believe never exceeded 471 fince the time of our being called out in the month of

* They are allowed to take fufficient air and exercife in the *day.*

† I mean by non-effectives fuch men as do not mount guard, &c. of which clafs at this time there are 140, many of whom however are returned as *effective* by the commanding officer.

January

January 1793—out of which upwards of 170 men
have been under my care fince the 15th of January, 1794.

This, I think, may be accounted for in two
ways. Firft, from the *foldiery* being expofed to
the *night damps*, which in confequence of feveral
arms of the fea and the neighbouring marfhes,
are very confiderable, and from which the *prifoners* are in a great meafure fecured by the prifons
being fhut up at a very early part of the evening.
Secondly, from the *flagrant abufes* which are fuffered to exift in the recruiting of *our* Militia by
which the Regiments are filled with a *motley fet*,
compofed of *raw young boys, difeafed refugees*, and
decrepid old men. Thus verifying the too well
founded remark of the humorift, and inftead of
being the *pillars* do actually become the *caterpillars*
of the nation*.

* A Striking, but *melancholy* inftance of this, exifts at this
moment in the Regiment to which I belong, where inftead
of 534 *duty men* (which is the proper compliment of the

The

The blood, we have remarked, retains a portion of the *carbonic acid* which may be useful in the fyftem as an *antifeptic*, fince it has long been known to poffefs the peculiar property of preferving animal fubftances, retarding their putrifaction, and even reftoring them to a found and frefh ftate, after the putrifactive procefs has begun to take place. Hence the utility of waters impregnated with this acid, given pretty largely in putrid, or bilious fevers, in difeafes of the lungs, and in fome kinds of ulcers, &c. May not a fomewhat peculiar to *oxygene* give rife to that principle which authors treat of under the denomination of the vitality of the blood ?

In the courfe of this work we fhall endeavour to fhew that many confiderable alterations in the fyftem take place, from the different quantities of

Regiment) we have never had more than 350, and while I am writing this, (*March* 1ft,) there are *only* 331 duty men, 63 *wanting to complete* and 140 non-effectives.—But of this we fhall fpeak more fully hereafter.

oxygene

oxygene contained in the blood; and many phenomena tend to evince that this principle is of infinite importance, nay even indifpenfibly neceffary
to the *continuance* of animal life.

A kind of volatile *vapour* or exhalation is continually flying off from the *warm blood*, which has a
fort of fœtid fmell, intermediate between that of
fweat and urine; this vapour after collection and
condenfation in convenient veffels, is of an aqueous
nature, partaking fomewhat of an alkaline quality; and fometimes by the flow return of the venous blood to the heart, thefe vapours ftagnate in
the cellular membrane, producing ædematous
fwellings in weak people. After the vapour is
diffipated, the blood of a healthy perfon congeals
into a trembling fciffile mafs. This exhalation
takes place immediately on its being drawn from
the living animal, and a fenfible vapour flies off,
which Dr. Cullen calls the *halitus* of the blood,
and which, being diffipated by this exhalation,
leaves the mafs fomewhat lighter; according to

E.   the

the degree of heat to which it is expofed, the extent of furface influenced by the air, or different conditions of the blood at the time. It is the *ferofity* of the blood which is fuppofed to afford this fubtile vapour, which is more purgent in carnivarous than in graminivorous animals, and even inftances are not wanting in the annals of phyfic, in which it has proved fatal.

On chemical analyfis, Dr. Haller found it to be the fame as the matter of perfpiration; and this indeed is what we fhould have expected, for as neither the *halitus*, nor the matter of perfpiration are poffeffed of any obvious acid or alkaline qualities, their *fenfible* properties would feem evidently to depend on a highly attenuated oily matter, of which the principle of inflammability feems to be the chief ingredient. There is at leaft no doubt but this is the cafe with refpect to *perfpiration*, as appears from the ftrong fcent that is conftantly fmelt after profufe fweats in fevers; and alfo from *dogs* being at all times able, by means of this

odour,

odour, not only to diftinguifh one fpecies of animal from another, but even any one *individual*
from every other of the fame fpecies.

By this evaporation of its thin, aqueous parts,
the neceffity of frequently taking food (particularly fluids) is encreafed, as by this evaporation
the blood being naturally of a faline quality, acquires an acrimonious putrefcency, the irritation
of which is faid to be the caufe of the frequency
of pulfe in fevers ; and the diffipation being encreafed according to the heat of the body and the
motion of the heart and arteries, nature ftrenuouf-
ly demands a recruit of the watery parts, by which
the cohefive parts of the blood are feparated from
each other, and are prevented from running together into a folid mafs ; for drink dilutes the *cobe-
five diathefis* of the blood, hinders its putrefaction
and carries off by the emunctaries, fuch particles
as have already become noxious.

Hence

Hence the great ufe of diluent drinks in fevers, more efpecially in thofe which have a putrid tendency. And hence it is that a perfon may *fubfift* for a long time without *folid food* provided he is properly fupplied with *drink*; but without this laft, life fubfifts but for a few days. It has however been obferved that in fuch as have their blood *too thin*, the globuli cohere and form moleculæ or polypi. There is an acrid and fœtid water fometimes returned from the *fœces* into the blood; hence coftivenefs in fevers is hurtful, the affufion of this matter encreafing putrefaction.

The blood, in the healthy ftate, when firft drawn from the body, is *apparently* an homogenous fluid of a beautiful florid red colour, unctious to the touch, fomewhat fuponaceous, and of an infipid faline tafte; but which, foon after it is feparated from the veffels, is found to be an heterogenous aggregate; perhaps obfcurely organized, and which is compofed of feveral parts differing much

from

from each other in their chemical and phyſical properties.

By chemical analyſis the blood is found to contain many more ſubſtances than thoſe which are evident to our ſenſes from its ſimple and ſpontaneous ſeparation; all of which we ſhall examine in their proper places. But before we proceed to its analyſis, it may not be amiſs to ſay ſomewhat more concerning its phyſical properties, as colour, temperature, taſte, ſmell and peculiar conſiſtence; on which ſomething has already been offered.

By the microſcope we diſcover in the blood, red globules, which, when joined with the coagulable lymph, make that part by ſome called *cruor,* but more properly *craſſamentum,* and which, when broken, according to Lewenhoeck and Boerhaave, in their way through the ſmall paſſages, loſe their red colour, become yellow and afterwards white: ſo that, according to the Leyden Phyſician, a *red globule* is an aſſemblage of many ſmaller *white globules*

bules and derives its colour from aggregation only : but this Dr. Haller could neither obferve nor readily admit.

Thefe red globules have been confidered as an oily matter, thereby accounting for their globular appearance ; but Dr. Cullen thinks there is no direct proof of this, alledging their ready union with and diffufibility in water render it very improbable. That they contain a pitchy oil is doubtlefs, as may be fully proved by chemical analyfis ; hence I would ask, May not the alkaline falts which they contain facilitate their union with aqueous menftrua ?

They have been varioufly reprefented by different microfcopical obfervers ; fome have thought them fpherical and divifible into a determinate number of other fpheres, but others again have not obferved this divifibility ; by fome they have been faid to be oblate fpheroids, or lenticular ; while others again have fuppofed them annular ;

and

and they have even been confidered as a hollow vefficle: hence we may infer, that microfcopical obfervations are liable to great uncertainties.

If it be queftioned whether thefe are not lenticular particles of the fame kind with thofe which Lewenhoeck obferved in fifhes, and which have been lately difcovered in the human fpecies, we anfwer, that being confcious of the difficulty attending the determination of fo intricate a point, we chufe rather to leave that (at leaft for the prefent) to men of more experience and greater depth of judgment than hazard an hypothefis, which, if it did not elucidate the fubject, might only plunge us into greater perplexities, and from which it might be difficult to free us. Hewfon, however obferves, that the particles are flat, like a guinea; but waving all abftrufe theories and intricate difquifitions, we refer to his Treatife on the Blood, for their more particular defcription.

The

The rednefs of the blood is peculiar to the globules, and depends upon thefe *only*. The intenfe-
nefs of their colour and the proportion they bear
to the whole mafs increafes with the ftrength of
the animal, being very confiderably more abundant in the robuft than in the debilitated ftate.

Dr. Cullen fuppofes the variation of colour in
the common mafs of blood to depend entirely on
the differences of aggregation in thefe globules.
Their diameter is very fmall, not exceeding the
1-2000th of an inch; and, have been imagined
by fome anatomifts, to change their figure into
an oblong fhape, adapted to the capacity of the
veffels through which they pafs, but which Dr.
Haller could never obferve with fufficient certainty. Nor indeed can we readily admit of fuch
a fuppofition; for were this the cafe, and were
the globules poffeffed of this peculiar *organic* power, we fhould find them by this kind of affimu-
lation, pervading every the moft *minute* veffels in
the

the body, which no one I think has ever been able to obferve in a *natural and healthy ftate of the parts.*

Indeed there have been inftances of *red blood* paffing off by perfpiration, &c. but I would account for fuch peculiarities by a *morbid relaxation* of the *cutaneous veffels*, permitting fuch parts to pafs as would not enter them in a *healthy ftate*; or, by any increafed afflux of the fluids to particular parts, irritating the veffels, and thereby procuring a paffage to the red blood; (of which we have an inftance in inflammations of the *tunica conjunctiva* of the eye) rather than admit of fuch peculiar organization of the red globules.

The circumambient air has no doubt confiderable influence on thefe peculiarities, as by a diminution of its *denfity* and *preffure*, the blood has been often known to burft through the fkin, or from the lungs, &c. occafioning hæmorrhagies. Hence the impropriety of exploring the tops of *very high mountains*, on the fummits of which the

F air

air is fo fpecifically light, as (independent of the effects we have already enumerated) to be wholly unfit for the purpofes of refpiration*.

Thefe globules do not contain *air* as fome have imagined, as is demonftrable from their fpecific weight, which either in their fluid or folid ftate, is nearly an eleventh part heavier than water. They may be obtained by wafhing the craffamentum in water, and afterwards evaporating to drynefs, but under this procefs they fuffer a change of colour.

---

* *Very deep vallies* are equally unfavourable to health as *very high mountains*; the air in the *former* being loaded with *carbonic acid*, or fixed air, (fimilar to that noxious vapour found in certain caverns and fubterraneous paffages,) and other grofs matters exhaled from the furface of the earth, in much more confiderable quantities, than are to be met with in the more elevated regions of the atmofphere; which latter abounds more efpecially in *hydrogene gaz*. (See Fourcroy, Berkenhout, and others.)—And hence it is extremely danger-ous in people of very delicate habits expofing themfelves to any very *fudden* and confiderable alterations of the atmofphere.

They

They abound moſt in the *human body* and eſpecially in the muſcles, but are not eſſential to muſcular motion, as we may readily infer from the muſcles of fiſh being *white*, and thoſe of rabbits, and ſome fowls nearly ſo.

The blood, while hot and in motion, remains conſtantly fluid; but if it be not kept fluid by the attrition of *vital circulation*, and is ſuffered to reſt in a moderate degree of cold, it takes the form of a ſolid maſs, which gradually and ſpontaneouſly ſeparates into two parts, as it likewiſe does by the addition of *alkahol, mineral acids, fermented liquors*, &c. Some Authors* have remarked that by agitation till cold, it will continue fluid. There are certain ſtates of the body no doubt, in which the coheſive powers of the fluids are conſiderably *diminiſhed* or even *deſtroyed*; but from what I have uniformly been able to obſerve, I do not heſitate to affirm

* Vide Nicholſon's Firſt Principles of Chemiſtry, p. 511.

that

that in a *difeafed ftate only*, will the blood be prevented from coagulating by *mere conquaffation*. It will
coagulate by a degree of heat equal to 150° of Farenheit's fcale ; but it will not coagulate by heat*
lefs than 120°. Hence Mr. Cline affirms that coagulation never takes place in fevers, obferving that
the heat in the higheft fever never exceeds 112° :
but how he could afcertain the exact heat of the
blood, while moving in its proper veffels, and in
all the varieties of conftitution and difeafe, I muft
confefs, I am at a lofs to determine.

The fpontaneous feparation and caogulation of
the blood frequently takes place in the laft mo-
ments of life ; it fometimes coagulates in the veins
of *living perfons*, and is found clotted in wounds
of the arteries†.

* Perhaps the blood, when it has not been expofed to the
action of the air, as in drawing it from the body, may not
require fo great heat as 120° to effect its coagulation.

† In a firm healthy conftitution as foon as the difcharge of
blood, which naturally accurs in every large wound, is over,

This

This is fully proved in amputations, after which, a confiderable portion of the capacity of the arteries is obliterated by the formation of coagulum, which in time becomes perfectly organized. A very curious cafe of this nature was related to me by Mr. Eligie, formerly Surgeon with the army in Flanders, during the heat of action a man was wounded in the leg, and amputation was performed, the Surgeon had fecured the *principal veffels*, but, apprehenfive of being taken prifoner, he had hurried on the dreffings and bandages in a very loofe manner, fo that when the man was creeping to fome adjoining bufhes in order to fhelter himfelf, the whole of the bandage fell off, and he was under the necef-fity of covering the *stump* with the *skirts* of his *coat*,

the parts become covered with a vifcid coagulable effufion from the now retracted arteries; but in conftitutions of an oppofite nature, where the folids are much relaxed the blood is generally in fuch a diffolved ftate as to afford no fecretion of this nature, and in order to fupply as much as poffible this deficiency, many artificial balfams have been applied.

yet

yet, notwithſtanding his being expoſed to the cold and rain for twenty-four hours before he was removed to the hoſpital, the man recovered and did well, without any further hæmorrhage taking place*. Trifling as this circumſtance may appear to ſome, it has ſaved the life of a ſoldier— It may do ſo again—and would induce us (independent of other cogent reaſons) to *reprobate* the man, who through motives of ſelf-intereſt, can ſtoop to rob the needy ſoldier of that *little*, which the bounty of his King hath given him; equally regardleſs of the ſoldiers ſufferings, or the *mandates of his Sovereign.*

In the veins of a living perſon, and in one dying of a fever, the blood has been ſeen, by the violence of the diſorder, changed into

* It may be remarked, that the men's cloathing in the Weſt Middleſex Regiment, in many inſtances, has not covered their loins, therefore could not afford ſo ſalutary a relief in caſe of exigence—dictum ſat, &c.

a

a concreted tremulous jelly throughout all the veins; and I have more than once feen the cavities of the arteries completely filled with it, producing thofe concrete fubftances, which are found in the heart and large veffels, and have been frequently, but erroneoufly taken for po·lypi†.

This difpofition to coagulate even in the vef-fels, under particular circumftances, as *fyncope*, &c. affords us an ufeful practical hint in cafes of internal hæmorrhagy ; as from the *lungs*, *uterus*, &c. when if the patient faints we ought not to endeavour to revive him by the application of any *volatile*, *foetid*, or *ftimulating* medicines, as is ufual-ly done, but rather fuffer him to remain in a ftate of fyncope for the fpace of five, ten, or even fif-teen minutes, by which time the mouths of the

---

† Sometimes coagulable lymph may by inflammation be poured out, forming a polypus during life; but we are in-clined to believe that *many* of thofe concretions which au-thors have mentioned as polypi, are formed after death.

bleeding

bleeding veffels, will be fhut up by contraction
or the formation of coagulum at their extremities.

The time the blood takes in coagulating is
different according to various circumftances in
the ftate of the individual from whence it is taken, as, in general, it coagulates fooner in weak
people than in thofe of a contrary habit, whofe
blood does not coagulate fo readily, but is when
coagulated a much more compact mafs.

In operations I have obferved with others, that
the blood coagulates *foonest* when the patient is
faint and emaciated, than in a ftrong healthy
fubject. The mode of extracting it will alfo
have a confiderable influence on its concertion.

Blood when in an inflamed ftate is thinner, coagulates flower, and is, when coagulated, more
firm than ordinary.

In

In general, after having ftood for about four minutes, it begins to coagulate and extends on the fides of the veffels till the procefs is completed, which is ufually the cafe in about ten minutes from its commencement. This coagulation is not entirely owing to cold or reft, for though it be kept in motion by any mechanical means, this phenomena is not prevented, though it may perhaps require a greater length of time in taking place; nor again, is expofure to air (though very favourable to this procefs) abfolutely neceffary, for when difcharged from the veffels into the cellular membrane it very foon coagulates as we frequently fee in bruifes, a remarkable inftance of which came under the obfervation of Mr. Cline; A woman who had fallen from a great height, was fent immediately to St. Thomas's hofpital; a great extravafation had taken place into the labia pudendi into which he made feveral punctures with a lancet, but no blood efcaped, though the accident had happened but a few minutes.

G

Mr.

Mr. Hewfon made a great number of experiments in order to determine on what caufe the coagulation of the blood depended ; he expofed the jugular vein of a rabbit and made a ligature at each end, yet the blood did not coagulate, though kept in perfect reft, but by mixing air with the blood by means of a third ligature, it coagulated in fifteen minutes, which clearly demonftrates, that air has great influence in producing this change. Again, on applying a ligature on the arm and making the puncture an hour afterwards, blood will flow out perfectly fluid. Hence it would feem probable that the blood-veffels in fome unknown manner preferve the blood in a ftate of fluidity, for while in the veffels and in a healthy ftate, it will not coagulate, though expofed to circumftances favourable to that change. In fome inftances it has been found incapable of coagulating without the admixture of fome *extraneous* fubftances. This, Dr Hunter particularly remarked in game that were hunted to death, as deer, &c. His experiments and obfervations were

ren-

rendered much more conclufive, by a man who died fuddenly in a paffion, being exhaufted of life by exceffive action, it thickened a little like cream, but a perfect coagulation by no means took place, the Doctor thinks it owing to a deprivation or change of fome of its natural qualities*.

If after blood is drawn, it is kept in a natural ftate of heat, it more readily coagulates, but this may be prevented by the addition of neutral falts. This natural difpofition in the blood to take a concrete form, is productive of various appearances and phenomena in difeafes, as coagula in aneurifms, &c. If a portion of aneurifmal coagulum be macerated in water, it will feparate into ftrata, which may be accounted for by the flow accumulation of coagulum in the aneurifmal fac ; layer fucceeding to layer, forming a laminated

---

* May not this arife from a deficiency of *oxygene* in the atmofphere, or an exhauftion of this principle during vioent exercife?

ftruc-

ftructure, which continues to encreafe fo long as
the fac is capable of any further diftention.—
Thefe membranous ftrata I have obferved both in
the encyfted and diffufed fpecies of eneurifm.
Hence we may readily account for the *firmnefs*
which fome parts of the aneurifmal fac. acquire,
in the more advanced ftages of the difeafe*. The
cohefion of thefe ftrata will be broken down by
maceration, and they may then be feparated.

The *craffamentum* of blood when forced from its
watery parts, is inflammable; and in a *healthy
ftate* of the animal it exceeds, or at leaft equals, the
quantity of *ferum*, which laft, in laborious people,
often occupies no more than one third of the mafs;

* It may not be unworthy of remark that, as blood-letting
when not accurately performed, is perhaps the moft frequent
caufe of this troublefome and often fatal difeafe, it were to
be wifhed. practitioners in general would pay more attention
to this nice and important operation.

and

and is fometimes diminifhed to a fourth or filth part in fevers*.

The blood in a perfectly found healthy ftate, free from putrefaction, and in a proper degree of heat, is neither *acid* nor *alkaline*, but mild and ge-latinous, fomewhat faltifh to the tafte. It is how-ever rendered acrid by difeafe, as in the waters of *dropfies*, which are frequently *alkaline*; and in fome cafes it approaches very near to a ftate of putre-faction; as in the *fcurvy*, where it frequently be-comes fo acrid as to corrode the veffels which contain it.

I have often remarked the furface of fcorbutic ulcers overfpread with a confiderable portion of dark, grumous blood; and it has been a general obfervation of moft authors who have written on

* Hence the utility of diluent drinks, given copioufly in moft kinds of fevers, as mentioned in a former part of this treatife.

the

the fubject, that the blood of *hæmorrhagies* in thofe who were afflicted with the *fcurvy,* was always of a more deep colour than ufual, inclining to black, and in many inftances incapable of complete coagulation[†].

That thefe peculiarities arife in a great meafure from inactivity and a confequent deprivation, or want of fome active principle neceffary to the welfare of the fyftem, feems evident from the remarks of Dr. Trotter, who, fpeaking of the fcurvy on board an *African slave-ship,* fays " Few " of the boys had any fcorbutic fymptoms : none " of them were fhakled, and by being allowed to " run about the deck, and occafionally affift in the " duty of the fhip their health feemed to be pre- "ferved by the exercife[*]." Whereas it feldom

---

[†] Vide Dr. Sandifort's cafe of the *blue boy,* as related by him in the Obfervations Anatomica—Pathologicæ Lugd. Batav. 1777 from p. 11.

[*] Vide Trotter on the Scurvy, Edit. 1792, p. 63.

failed

failed to attack thofe who were moft *corpulent* and had taken the leaft exercife, infomuch that the fame juftly celebrated author obferves that, " So " general was this obfervation, and fo fully was " I confirmed of it that when a negro was becom- " ing rapidly fat, it was no difficult matter to de- " termine how foon he would be feized with the " fcurvy." This peculiar dark colour of the blood in perfons affected with the fcurvy, may in a great meafure depend on the want of oxygene*, and this feems to be ftill more confirmed by the colour of the blood in *confumptive patients* being fo univerfally oppofite to that in the *fcurvy.*

While a pupil at the General Hofpital near Not-tingham, I had daily opportunities of examining

---

* This fuppofition I believe firft occured to Dr. Beddoes of Oxford, whofe obfervations on the fcurvy, &c. have exhibited a more valuable collection of important facts, than hath perhaps been *ever* offered to the philofophical world in fo fmall a compafs.

the

the blood of phthifical patients and found it univerfally of a *bright red*, inclining fomewhat to
purple, and generally exhibiting a very large portion of inflammatory cruft when coagulated. This
again differs much from the colour of the blood
in perfons who, from trifling complaints or more
frequently from *habitude*, have been let blood; in
whom it is generally of an intermediate colour
between the *very dark*, and that of a more *bright
red*, than that which is ufually underftood by the
appellation of *florid**.

This difference of colour, feems to hold in the
more folid parts, as I have frequently remarked
when examining the bodies of fuch as have died
of fcurvy, or phthifis. In the former I do not
remember to have feen *one inftance* where the mufcles did not univerfally appear of a morbid *dark*

---

* It may be remarked that the blood of pregnant women,
I have frequently obferved to be *extremely dark*, though *not
always* fo.

colour ;

colour; whereas in the latter I as uniformly found them of a *bright red*. Hence the impropriety of exhibiting oxygéne in cafes of phthifis as recommended by fome; when it is more than probable that its fuperabundance will not a little contribute to the difeafe.

And I am inclined to believe that a ftill lefs quantity in the air we breath would be found in general more beneficial*. The quantity of heat difengaged from it being fo great, that were the atmofphere furcharged with this principle, which in a *certain quantity*† is fo eminently ferviceable for the purpofes of life, the circulation would be rendered *too* rapid, and the excefs of heat become fo confiderable, as to produce fymptoms equally or

---

* Vide Dr. Beddoes Obfervations on *Confumptions*, &c.

† M. Lavoifier has fixed the quantity of vital air in the atmofphere at about 28 parts in 100 —This however will vary according to fituation.

per-

perhaps more prejudicial than could poffibly ac-
crue from the want of it.

That air is contained in the fluids of the human body, I believe, is very generally allowed ;
and is fully proved from the phenomena exhibited
by animals in an exhaufted receiver, but how it
arrives there has been a matter of confiderable
difpute, nor is it effential to our purpofe, that we
fhould examine minutely into the fubject. Many
have fuppofed that it was introduced along with
our aliments *alone* ; others that it was more frequently abforbed from the lungs in the paffage of
the blood through thofe organs, while others
again as confidently affert that it never comes in
contact with the blood in the lungs. But the difcoveries of modern philofophers have taught us
far otherwife ;---the anatomift can now readily
demonftrate thofe innumerable pores and foramina, to be obferved along the courfe of the
larynx, afpera arteria, and bronchia ; while the
modern chemift fpurning the ignorant filence of
alchemy,

alchemy, and emulative of cotemporary merit, labours to cull the *genuine* phenomena of nature,
rejecting the flimfy arguments of the *mere theorift*,
and ever indefatigable in his refearches, feems as
it were by flow degrees emerging from the fhades
of that impenetrable darknefs which, till late, was
wont to be the veil of explication and of truth.

" Amicus Cicero, Amicus Plato, fed magis amicus veritas."

Thefe mifts feem already to be difpelled, and
we are now convinced that upon the diverfity of
thefe pores or foramina, both with refpect to number, condition, and mucus with which they may be
covered, as well as the fize of the refpiratory organs, depends the reafon why each individual con-
not inhale and abforb the fame quantity of falubrious matter from one and the fame air. Hence
we may readily infer that many difeafes have been
fuppofed to originate from a vitiated or imperfect
ftate of the atmofphere, which with greater juftice
might have been applied to a default in the ftate

of

of perfection of thofe organs deftined for the feparation of the more falutary principles of the atmofphere.

The celebrated profeffor of Gottingen* feems
to have been aware of the connection between
refpiration and the ftate of the blood in animals ;
as appears from his notes to Haller's phyfiology,
where he fays " Among the ufes of refpiration, is
" that of reforption ; by which the veffels of the
" lungs abforb from the air inhaled in infpiration,
" not only vapours mixed with the air, but min-
" gle with our humours by means of the forami-
" na, ducts and proper canals, fome other *more*
" *noble parts*, conftituting at the fame time one of
" the elements of the air." And in note 72, he
fays " If, in a few words, I might offer my opi-
" nion about the air found in our bodies which
" has been the bafis of fo many difputes, I am
" perfuaded, that atmofpheric air is a very com-

* Wrifberg.

" pound

"pound fluid, confifting of parts, very different
"in their nature and quality ; which parts, when
" mixed with any primogenial fluid as a vehicle,
" make the common air we inhale in infpiration.
" This primogenial fluid is perhaps, that air
" which we obferve in animals, vegetables, and
" likewife in the earth itfelf, differing only accord-
" ing to the various fubftances with which it is
" united. If there is mixed in a due proportion
" with this univerfal fluid, any elaftic ethereal,
" electric principle, or any particles not yet fully
" underftood, perhaps there will refult falubrious
" atmofpheric air. But it will become infected
" and noxious in various degrees, from an admix-
" ture of putrefactive fubftances, narcotic or in-
" flammable fuffocating elements. For that rea-
" fon it feems to me very proper that our judge-
" ment refpecting the falutary or noxious quality
" of the air, fhould be directed by thefe princi-
" ples ; and hence it will be in our power to
" correct unwholefome air, provided we know
" what qualities the air fhould poffefs, as moft
" fuited

" fuited to the function of refpiration." The fame
ingenious author thought this *electric principle* (as
he fuppofed it to be,) might influence the tone
and irritability of the fibres of the body, as alfo
the *caufes* and *increafe* of animal heat—And the
difcoveries of modern chemiftry feem to warrant
our opinion, in fuppofing the conclufions of profeffor Wrisberg will eventually be confirmed with
but a very trivial alteration in terms.

This principle by modern chemifts has been
denominated oxygene, and is now fuppofed by
fome ingenious phyfiologifts to be the principal
agent by which the vital organs are excited to the
performance of their feveral functions, and without which thefe muft not only ceafe, but even
fuffer very material alterations in their mechanical
ftructure. Sed " nullius exitium patitur natura
" videri;" hence fhe hath furnifhed us with fuch
principles as are beft fuited for the purpofes of
life and organization; and hath fo varied the proportions of each in our atmofphere, as to adapt it

in

in a very particular manner to all the several varieties of conftitution and difeafe ; and it is by accepting the important hint fhe hath given us, that we have fo lately added to our ftock of chemical and phyfiological knowledge, and by a profecution of which we may one day hope to reduce the empiricifm of medicine, and eftablifhed a more beneficial practice, on the more enlightened principles of pneumatic chemiftry. Efforts have been made, and thofe not puerile ones, by Beddoes, Girtanner, Goodwyn*, and others, in order to afcertain and eftablifh the influence of oxygene, in the animal œconomy. From them we learn that the laws of irritability, and almoft every phenoma attendant on animal life, in a great meafure depends on the prefence of this principle. Dr. Goodwyn's experiments are fo fimple, and at

* Vide Goodwyn's Connection of Life with Refpiration, a work, which though fmall, is neverthelefs pregnant with many important obfervations drawn from experiments equally diftinguifhed for their aptnefs of inftitution, and the accuracy with which they were made.

the

the fame time fo fully adequate to explain its influence on mufcular motion, that a reference to
his tract, would fuperfede the neceffity of quoting
them here, but as his obfervations may not have
been feen by fome of my readers, I am the more
willing to enhance the value of this work with an
abftract of his remarks on this fubject. Speak-
ing of fome experiments, by artificial inflation,
for afcertaining the connection between refpiration
and the colour of the blood, and between the
blood and contractions of the heart, he fays " In
" all the examples, I obferved that when the blood
" which paffed into the left auricle was florid, the
" auricle and ventricle contracted ftrongly, and
" the circulation went on *as in health* ; but when
" the blood began to put on a fhade of *brown*, the
" contractions were diminifhed ; and when it was
" *black* the contractions ceafed, although the auri-
" cle was diftended with blood ; and as the con-
" tractions ceafed the functions of the body were
" fufpended ; but as foon as the florid colour was
" reftored, the auricle and ventricle refumed their
" con-

" contractions, and they gradually recovered their
" natural ftate; and all the other functions re-
" turned.

" In thefe examples the contraction of the left
" auricle and ventricle are immediately affected by
" the *quality* of the blood paffing into them ; for
" when they ceafe, the auricle is filled with black
" blood ; but notwithftanding thefe facts, to fuch
" as have particular opinions about the manner in
" which the blood acts upon the heart, it may not
" appear clear that thefe alterations in the con-
" tractions arofe from the quality of the blood
" *alone.* This difficulty, however may be removed
" by attending to fimilar experiments in the am-
" phibious animals, where the heart has only one
" auricle and ventricle, where the pulmonary ar-
" tery is a fmall branch from the aorta, and the
" pulmonary vein proportionably fmall empties
" itfelf into the finus venofus and auricle, along
" with the vena cava afcendens, which carries the
" principal part of the blood. Here the quantity

I   of

" of blood brought by the vena cava would be
" fufficient to keep up the action of the heart, in-
" dependent of the pulmonary circulation, if quan-
" tity alone were required ; and the coats of the
" finus venofus and auricle, as well as thofe of
" the blood-veffels, are almoft tranfparent : the
" lungs alfo contain a quantity of air fufficient
" to furnifh the neceffary chymical changes to
" the pulmonary blood for a *confiderable time* with-
" out any communication with the atmofphere ;
" fo that the alterations which take place in the
" colour of the blood, and in the motions of the
" heart, in confequence of obftructed refpiration,
" are more gradual and diftinct, than in the ani-
" mals with double hearts, in which all the blood
" paffes through the lungs.

" I confined a large living toad on a plate of
" metal, with his belly upwards ; then I removed
" a part of the fternum, and his heart and lungs
" were expofed to view. The lungs were then
" filled with air ; the blood in the pulmonary
" veins

" veins was florid, and the heart contracted *forty-*
"*four* times in a minute. In this state he was
" immerfed in a fmall quantity of tranfparent wa-
" ter, where the alterations in the colour of the
" blood and in the contractions of the heart, could
" be accurately diftinguifhed. When he had re-
" mained in the water fifteen minutes, the blood in
" the lungs began to put on a dark colour, and
" the contractions of the heart were diminifhed to
" *thirty.* In fifteen minutes more the dark colour
" of the blood was increafed, and the contrac-
" tions of the heart were *eighteen.* The animal
" now made feveral ftruggles to relieve itfelf, and
" threw fome air out of its lungs ; but the pulmo-
" nary blood becoming ftill more dark coloured,
" the contractions of the heart were diminifhed
" ftill farther, and in *forty minutes* more they
" ceafed ; although the finus venofus and auricle,
" and the trunk of the vena cava, were filled with
" black blood. The animal was now removed
" from the water, without any figns of life ; but
" before the expiration of *two minutes* he opened
his

" his mouth and took a large quantity of frefh
" air into his lungs. Soon after he emptied them
" almoft entirely ; and this was repeated feveral
" times. During the procefs, the blood in the
" pulmonary veins began to be florid, and the
" heart to renew its contractions ; and in *fifteen*
" *minutes* from the firft inflation the contractions
" of the heart were *thirty-five,* all the functions
" were recovered and he walked about without any
" expreffions of uneafinefs,

" This experiment was repeated feveral times
" on the fame toad ; and fometimes when he did
" not fill his lungs, after being removed from the
" water, we injected fome air into them with a
" blow-pipe, and preffed it out afterwards, in imi-
" tation of the example he had given us ; and by
" thefe means we renewed the contraction of the
" heart feveral times. But at length he was re-
" moved from the water, and fuffered to remain
" an hour before frefh air was injected into his
" lungs. Soon after it was injected the blood in
" the

" the pulmonary veins become florid; but the
" heart did not again renew its contractions."

These experiments he repeated on the lizard;
and in every case the contractions of the heart
were less frequent, in proportion as the pulmonary blood became darker, and vice versa. And
though in every example the quantity of blood
which flowed to the heart was sufficient to keep
up its contractions, yet still were they gradually
diminished in proportion to the dark colour of
the blood; and so as that, when it was *black*, they
ceased altogether. Hence he very naturally infered that from the *quality* of the blood *alone* could
arise these alterations in the motion of the heart.
And that the *chymical quality which the blood acquires
in passing through the lungs, is necessary to keep up the action of the heart, and consequently the health of the body.*

From hence he drew those remarks on the nature and effects of *submersion* and *strangulation,*
and on the cure of these diseases; as must be e-
qually

qually important to the man of humanity as to
the medical practitioner, and the intrinsic value
of which cannot be too highly esteemed by every
useful member of the community.

It were much to be wished that the investigation of these, and other similar phenomena, were
more universally imparted to mankind. than can
possibly be expected through the medium of *medical publications*, which are, in general, supposed
to be full of theoretical disquisitions, too abstruse
for the understanding of any man who is not versed
in the science of medicine.—Perhaps, if delivered
to the world as matter of curiosity, it might excite
more effectually the active spirit of enquiry, and
rouse the benevolent exertions of philanthropy, to
prevent the dangerous *monopoly* of science.

The opinions of Doctors Beddoes and Girtanner
seem evidently to confirm those of Dr. Goodwyn;
but they go still further and suppose the solid fibre
acquires its faculty of irritability from the oxygene

gene which the lungs and circulation of the fluids are continually fupplying ; and that unlefs the action of ftimuli applied to the irritable fibre, be fufficiently ftrong to carry off any furplus of this irritable principle, the fibre will become furcharged therewith, and that equilibrium neceffary to its moft perfect ftate will be deftroyed : while, on the other hand, a total or irreparable exhauftion of this principle from the fibre deftroys its faculty of irritability ; as in the cafe of gangrene. The fibre fuffers a change of colour, becoming dark and afterwards *black* ; fubject to the laws of inorganized matter, beginning to decompofe and putrefy.

A very powerful ftimulus will, in a very fhort time, reduce the fibre to this ftate. Such, for inftance, is the ftate of the fibre in animals killed by very ftrong poifons, by the bite of the rattlefnake ; in animals deftroyed by a knife dipped in the juice of the aconite, or by poifoned arrows. The fame effects will be produced by weak ftimuli

muli (though in a more gradual manner) when
conftantly acting upon one part of the fyftem,
fuch as *flow poifons*, the abufe of fpiritous liquors,
&c. which in the end exhaufts the whole fyftem
and produces death. Hence we are led to fay
with Cicero " Arteria animam accipit è pulmo-
nibus."

By putrefaction, expofure to air, or a long continued heat equal to 96° of Fahrenheit's fcale, the
whole mafs of blood, but more efpecially the ferum, is converted into a very fætid liquor, firft
the ferum, and afterwards, but more flowly, the
red cruor, till at length both it and the ferum
leaving very few fæces behind, is diffipated in the
form of a volatile fætid exhalation. The blood
becomes fætid when a little diffolved by beginning
putrefaction, at the fame time affuming an alkaline quality, which is again deftroyed in the advanced ftage of putrefcency.

Putrid

Putrid blood cannot be infpiffiated by any means with which we are acquainted, and its refolution is extremely difficult, after having been coagulated by rectified fpirits. By expofure to a regular and continued, gentle heat, it undergoes the putrid fermentation. When heated more ftrongly it coagulates, gradually dries and, as De Haen has difcovered, lofes $\frac{7}{8}$ of its weight and effervefces with acids; and by a well managed fire, it may be hardened into a corneous, bony, or even ftony fubftance.

The colour of the blood becomes brighter and deeper, by the addition of neutral or fixed alkaline falts, both of which produce almoft fimilar effects without either thickening or rendering the blood more fluid. The volatile alkalies give it a brown tinge, and coagulate it, which laft phenomena takes place alfo by the admixture of rectified fpirits, diftilled oils, or vinegar*. As far as my own

---

* Anatomifts have faid that the deep colour of the blood of the chick in egg, arofe folely from the deep feat of the vein; but from many experiments I am warranted in

experiments

experiments and the affertions of others lead me to infer it does not effervefce with any falt.

A weak acid fcarcely alters it, but the ftronger ones coagulate it immediately, producing a change, of colour. By filtrating, and evaporating the fil- trated liquor to drynefs, over a gentle fire and afterwards lixiviating the refidual matter we may obtain fuch neutral falts, as each acid forms with falt of Soda*.

The blood contains in its fubftance a confidera- ble quantity of marine falt, which is evident to the tafte, and fometimes even vifible by the micro- fcope, thefe faline particles are faid to be more abundant in its moft ferous parts. May not the prefence of thefe faline particles in the gaftric juice, contribute much to the diffolution of our aliments, and be otherwife ferviceable in ftimulat- ing the veffels ? That it contains earth is eafily

afferting, that the chick has no fooner breathed, than its blood becomes more florid.

* Vide Fourcroy's Elem. Chem. &c.

demonftrated

demonſtrated from chemical analyſis, and from the phenomena of nutrition; it is principally found in the moſt fluid, and more eſpecially in the oleaginous parts of the blood, it conſtitutes about a 150th part of the whole maſs, containing ſome ferruginous particles attracted by the magnet; its quantity is continually increaſing, in proportion as the nutritious parts of our food abounds with it, whereby the brittleneſs of the bones, and hardneſs of every other part is increaſed, it being every where depoſited in the cellular texture and more eſpecially in the coats of the arteries, producing cruſts, at firſt callous, but which afterwards, aſſume a bony or even ſtony nature; as is frequently ſeen in the beginning of the aorta in perſons far advanced in years, and the valves of this artery have been found covered with chalky concretions, which by preventing them from performing their office, kept the left ventricle of the heart conſtantly overcharged with blood, diſtending it to twice its natural ſize, inducing a marked debility in the animal functions, and thereby

by dropfy. I have likewife found thefe depofi-
tions of calcareous earth and offification of the
coats of this artery in cafes of aneurifm.

It is the depofition and accumulation of this
earth, between the primœval fibres of a bone,
which conftitute and finifh the procefs of offification ; but which being reabforbed and conveyed
into the circulating mafs, as is fometimes the cafe,
may give rife to the above mentioned and perhaps many other difeafes, as may be inferred
from a confideration of the nature of the gouty
earth, biliary concretions, calculi, &c. The abundance of this is perhaps the worft quality which
our humours can poffefs. And this encreafed
hardnefs and rigidity of the whole animal body,
diminifhing the mufcular powers, and debilitating
the fenfes, conftitute *old age*. An evil, alas ! which
fooner or later attends every mortal, who is not
cut off by other premature means. Its acceffion
is earlier in thofe who have been fubjeɛted to hard
labour, or violent exercife ; or in thofe who have
given

given themfelves up to pleafure in every criminal excefs, living upon unwholefome diet, and ufing indifcriminately and freely the moft inebriating liquors; than in thofe who on the contrary, have ever ftrictly adhered to a moderate or abftemious courfe of life, ufing temperance in every thing, and cautioufly avoiding every baneful influence: or in fuch as have removed from a cold to a warm climate.

By fome late experiments a confiderable quantity of metallic calx has been found in the blood, when calcined, and which is eafily reducible by any matter which has a ftronger affinity with oxygene than the metal with which it was combined.

That air is contained in the blood in an unelaftic ftate, and that too in a very confiderable quantity, is proved by putrefaction and diftillation, or by its expanfion in an exhaufted receiver; though as I have remarked we are not to fuppofe

pofe that the red globules are bubbles full of air, as their being fpecifically heavier than the ferum is fufficient to refute any argument, which may be advanced in fupport of fuch an opinion.

Chemiftry has in various ways elucidated the nature of the blood. When firft drawn, and diftilled with a flow heat, before the putrefactive procefs commences, it yields an aqueous fluid to the quantity of five parts in fix of the whole mafs ; poffeffing very little tafte or fmell, till towards the finifhing of the operation, when it becomes more or lefs charged with a very fœtid oil. This aqueous fluid very readily putrifies.

The refidual matter when expofed to a ftronger heat yields different alkaline liquors, the firft of which being fætid, acrid, and inclining to a red colour, has been ufually called the fpirit of the blood, confifting of a volatile falt with a fmall proportion of oil, held in folution by water, to the amount of about 1-20th part of the original mafs.

An

An acrimonious liquor very fimilar to this may be extracted from the fat, as alfo from putrid flefh and blood—It contains a fmall proportion of marine falt.

Somewhat fooner, and along with the oil, there arifes a dry volatile falt, adhering to the neck and fides of the glafs in branchy flakes, but in a very fmall quantity, amounting only to about an *eigh-tieth* part of the whole mafs.

The oil which comes over next is at firft yellow, afterwards blackifh, and at laft bears a great refemblance to pitch, being exceedingly acrid and inflammable; and in the proportion of about one *fiftieth* part of the whole mafs. The refiduum left in the bottom of the retort is a porous inflammable coal or cinder, which burns and leaves afhes behind; and from which by ablution with water, a mixed falt may be obtained, compofed partly of marine falt, and partly of fixed alkalies, with a fmall quantity of fixed earth. This fixed

falt

falt does not occupy more than about one *five hundredth* part of the original mafs, and of which only *one fourth* is alkaline.

When calcined by an intenfe heat, it affords a fmall quantity of an acid fpirit, which is fuppofed to be owing partly to the marine falt in the blood, and partly to thofe parts of our vegetable aliments not yet animalized by digeftion* ; and from this laft we may underftand how an acid may be procured from the blood of graminivorous animals as well as from that of man.

By diftillation on a water bath, a phlegm of a faint fmell is afforded, which is neither acid nor

* The digeftive and affimilating powers of the animal œconomy are fitted to prepare from the aliments taken in, a fluid fuited to the purpofes of that œconomy, particularly for the nutrition of the more folid parts ; and fuch fluid, whilft in a condition fit for its purpofe, we prefume to be bland, mild, and nowife noxious or hurtful. But if there exift any morbid dificiency in the affimilating powers of digeftion, thefe qualities muft be fenfibly altered.

alkaline,

alkaline, but which by virtue of an animal fubftance it holds in folution, readily putrifies.—
Dried blood when expofed to the air flightly at-
tracts humidity, and in the courfe of a few months,
a faline efflorefcence is formed upon its furface,
which Rouelle difcovered to be falt of foda.
When diftilled with a naked fire it affords a
phlegm in the ftate of fal ammoniac, fuperfatu-
rated with fixed alkali. Weiuffens firft difcovered this empyreumatic acid, the nature of which has
excited fo many difputes among phyfiologifts, and
which has not hitherto been properly examined.
A light oil is afterwards forced over, fucceeded
by an oil more ponderous and coloured, and laftly
the thick oil with concrete volatile alkali; the refiduum in the form of a fpongy coal remains in the
retort, very difficult of incineration, containing
fea-falt, cretaceous foda, iron, and an earthy fubftance which is found to be calcareous phofphate.
Rouelle has beftowed much time and pains in examining the blood of different animals, and more
efpecially quadrupeds, as the ox, horfe, calf,

L   fheep,

fheep, hog, afs, and goat; he obtained the fame
products from all of them as from the human
blood, only in very different proportions.

By experiments made on the blood in its original ftate, we are not enabled to demonftrate the
nature of the component parts of this fluid;
but its fpontaneous decompofition and feparation
into two parts, the craffamentum and ferum, affords us different methods of accomplifhing this,
by a feparate examination of each fubftance. The
chemical analyfis of the blood was confined to
very narrow limits till within thefe few years,
when the labours of Minghini, Rouelle the
younger, Bucquet and others, threw a great light
upon the fubject, and by their experiments and
obfervations opened a vaft field for the inquifitive
chemift, anatomift, or phyfiologift to indulge the
luxuriancy of his imagination, and plainly evince
that by a fteady purfuit of thofe paths which they
have pointed out to us we may hope to arrive at
the greateft perfection in the analyfis of animal
matters,

matters, and from the obfervations and refearches of fuch learned men, joined to thofe facts which we have been able to collect, we fhall proceed to the confideration of the properties which characterize the different fubftances of which this heterogenous aggregate is compofed ; and firft of the ferum.

The *ferum* is a peculiar fluid, whofe chemical and phyfical properties, it is of great importance to underftand, and as by a careful examination of its conftituent parts, many very ufeful practical hints may be deduced, we fhall confider it at fome length.

It is not pure water as fome have fuppofed, but a tranfparent aqueous fluid, of a yellowifh green colour, denominated by fome authors the *albuminous* fluid. It is not as it would feem homogenous, and is fpecifically heavier than water by one *thirty-eighth* part, and the craffamentum is heavier than this fluid, by nearly *one twelfth*. It is found

floating

floating on the furface of the craffamentum, which it every way furrounds, the red cruor being as it were completely immerfed in it. It is of a dull brackifh tafte, and fomewhat unctious and adhefive. It coagulates and hardens by a heat much iefs than 212° degrees of Fahrenheit's thermometer, and will take a concrete form much harder than the craffamentum by the commixture of acids, or rectified fpirits, as alfo by a concuffive motion, forming firft an indiffoluble glue, afterwards a flefhy membranous fubftance, and at length fhrinks up to a corneous fubftance, or friable gum ; on preffing this coagulum, a fmall quantity of a ferous fluid diftils from it, which has been called the ferofity of the blood, and in which its neutral falts, or whatever occafions its faline tafte, are faid to refide.

When once coagulated it is incapable of becoming fluid again. When diftilled on the waterbath it gives over a mild infipid phlegm, neither acid nor alkaline, but which advances rapidly to putrefaction ;

putrefaction ; the refiduum is dry, hard and tranfparent like horn, no longer foluble in water, but
which, by a ftrong heat, gives over an alkaline
phlegm, a confiderable quantity of concrete volatile alkali, and an intenfely fœtid oil. All its
products are of a very difagreeable fœtid fmell.

The refiduum of this laft procefs is a coal very
difficult to incinerate, and which when diftilled
by a naked fire almoft fills the retort. It is fo
difficult to incinerate, that it cannot be reduced to
afhes, unlefs it is kept in a red heat for feveral
hours, with a large furface expofed to the air.
Thefe afhes are of a dark grey colour, containing marine falt, cretaceous foda, and fome calcareous phofphate.

When expofed in an open veffel to a warm temperature for a certain length of time, it foon putrifies, affording concrete volatile alkali of an
abominable fmell, in confiderable quantities. Its
putrefaction proceeds fo rapidly, as not to afford

Bucquet

Bucquet an opportunity of deciding whether it paffes to an acid ftate, before it becomes alkaline. It readily unites with water in any proportion, lofing its confiftence, tafte, and greenifh colour, but not perfectly unlefs their union is promoted by agitation, as their different denfities in fome meafure keeps them afunder. When poured into boiling water it in general coagulates inftantly. When diffolved in water it forms a white opake fomewhat milky fluid, which Bucquet fays poffeffes all the characteriftic properties of milk, as in affording cream, coagulating by heat, acids, &c. By the addition of alkalies it is rendered more fluid, as it were by a kind of folution.

Acids, as I have juft obferved have a directly oppofite effect, and form therewith a concrete ftubftance, which by filtration and evaporation affords fuch neutral falts, as the acid made ufe of forms with falt of foda, a fact which, beyond a doubt, proves the exiftence of falt of foda in the blood

blood, difengaged and poffeffed of all its properties.

The fubftance which this fluid forms by the
addition of acids is very readily diffoluble in volatile alkali, which is the proper folvent of the
albuminous part ; but it is far from being completely foluble in pure water. When united to
volatile alkali it may be decompofed and precipitated by the admixture of acids. It affords by
diftillation with a naked fire pretty near the fame
products as are obtained from dried ferum, and
its refiduum contains cretaceous foda in no incon-
fiderable quantity, from which Bucquet concludes,
that there is a portion of falt of foda fo intimately
combined in the ferum, as not to be completely
faturated by the coagulating acid.

The ferum by the action of the nitrous acid,
when expofed to a gentle heat, affords mephitis
and by the application of a greater heat to the mixture nitrous gas is fet at liberty ; the refidue affords

fords acid of fugar and a very fmall quantity of that peculiar acid, which M. de Morvéau calls the *malufian acid.*

The decompofition of metallic falt takes place very readily by the addition of ferum, which produces no fuch effect on the calcareous and argillaceous neutral falts. It is coagulable by alkali, as I have before remarked, and the coagulum produced by this union differs very confiderably from that formed by the action of acids, which laft is very difficultly foluble in water, but which, as Bucquet has difcovered, is not the cafe with fuch as is formed by rectified fpirits. Thefe are not the only phenomena in which thefe coagula differ. The ferum contains befides the coagulable albumen, a confiderable proportion of fimple water, and fome mucus, not fo eafily drawn into threads as the craffamentum, and not influenced by heat or acids, in a manner fimilar to this albumen.

A

A fecond kind of lymph has been difcovered by Hewfon, which was alfo obferved by Kraufius. The pleuritic crufts, polypi, and artificial membranes are, according to different anatomifts and phyfiologifts, formed from this part of the blood.

From the foregoing experiments therefore, we conclude, that the ferum is an animal mucilage, compofed of water, acidifiable oily bafes, marine falt, cretaceous foda, and calcareous phofphate. This laft was the fubftance which Fourcroy fuppof-ed to produce the rofe-coloured precipitate, which he obtained by the union of ferum and a folution of mercury in the nitrous acid. This appearance he obferved in many other animal fluids as well as the ferum. After the addition of mercurial ni-tre, and even of nitrous acid alone, producing a rofe or light flefh colour, though before fuch ad-dition the liquid was fcarcely coloured. This mucilage becoming concrete by the action of fire and acids, is a fingular property, and which be-fore any other merits the attention of phyficians,

M   Mr.

Mr. Scheele thinks the combination of heat produces this phenomena.

We have fhewn then, that from the ferum by
the agency of fire, pretty near the fame principles
may be extracted though in different proportions,
as from the craffamentum when obtained by fimilar proceffes ; yielding however much more water
but no iron at all. It would feem that thofe two
fecretions, faliva and mucus, have a great affinity
to ferum, as fimilar principles only with a lefs
proportion of oil and falt, and more abundant
aqueous parts, may be obtained from both thefe
humours.

. The coagulable parts of the ferum feem more
efpecially defigned for nutrition, and the thinner
juices fecreted from it, ferve various purpofes
highly ufeful to the animal œconomy ; fuch as
the diluting and affifting the diffolution of our
aliment, preferving the natural moifture of different parts, preventing the folids from becoming
rigid

rigid and inflexible, or from fuffering by abrafion
in the different motions of the body, which muft
have inevitably been the confequence, had not
our all-wife and even provident Creator prevented
their attrition by a fecretion of lubricating juices
proportioned to their different quantities of action.

Hence we fee various diforders take their rife
from either a fcarcely or abundance of thefe feveral fluids which, though, apparently, perhaps trifling in themfelves, yet when confidered in their
official capacity as a neceffary inftrument of human
exiftence, they become of infinite importance ; no
lefs fo perhaps (comparatively fpeaking) than the
more complicated organs fo effentially neceffary to
life ; and indeed we fee daily that any morbid de-
viations in the diftribution of thefe fluids produce
ultimately fimilar effects, as acrue from any preternatural influence exerted on the apparently more
important organs, for the *ultimate* confequences .
may be equally fatal, however widely the rapidity

dity of their progrefs, and the painful influence of their effects may differ : for no one would pronounce an animal healthy, when deprived, and in the actual want of any one natural quality of which it ought to be poffeffed ; fince it muft be obvious, that every the moft minute part of an animal, has a *proportionately* equal influence on the œconomy and welfare of the whole ; however trivial it may appear when confidered in an abftract point of view.

The ferum, according to Sir John Pringle, Mr. Gaber, and others, is that fubftance which alone is capable of producing *genuine pus* ; and not as Boerhaave, Platner, and many others are of opinion ; that it is formed by a diffolution of the blood-veffels, nerves, mufcles and other folids in the fluids of thofe parts in which inflammatory tumours occur : for it is evident from the experiments of Sir John Pringle* as well as thofe of Mr.

* Vide Apendix to his Treatife on Difeafes of the Army.

Gaber

Gaber related by himfelf in the fecond volume of the Acta Taurinenfia, that, far from affording good pus, the mixture of any of thefe fubftances, induces a degeneracy in the matter of ulcers. An opinion which feems highly probable, has been advanced with regard to the formation of pus from ferum, as by a degree of fermentation raifed upon the ferous parts of the blood after its fecretion into the cavities of ulcers and abfceffes, in confequence either of the natural heat of the parts or of heat artificially applied: and fome experiments of Sir John Pringle feem greatly to elucidate this opinion, for by expofing pure ferum in a furnace regulated to the human heat, he found, that in a few days, after becoming turbid, it depofited a white purulent fediment, but the craffamentum, under exactly fimilar circumftances, from a deep crimfon changed to a dark livid colour, which, when mixed with water, gave it a tawny hue, and which was the cafe with ferum when a few red globules were added to it, though digefted for the fame fpace of time, and in the fame degree

of

of heat. Mr Gaber's experiments all tend to elucidate and corroborate the fame opinion. Is it
not more efpecially the *coagulable lymph* or *albuminous* parts of the ferum from whence good
pus is generated*? All the ferum in the body has
been fometimes found white as milk, owing to a
fuperabundance of chyle ; this fubftance on being
mixed with the blood, does not immediately
change its nature, as is evident from milk being
afterwards made from it ; but after having cir-
culated through the body and been mixed with a
variety of animal juices, fomented with heat, it
undergoes a material alteration, part being depofited in the cellular texture under the form of
an unctious fubftance called fat, and which is
fometimes reabforbed ; a part is deftined for the
generation of red-globules, another portion changes into ferum, and its more fluid parts pafs off,
fome by urine and fome by perfpiration, a fmall

* Vide Bell on Ulcers, p. 60.

quantity

quantity being retained in the habit to dilute the blood.

We are now come to treat of that part of the blood which, after having ſtood for a certain length of time, ſpontaneouſly ſeparates from the ſerum, in which it ſinks, and takes the form of a tremulous coagulated maſs, called the *craſſamen-tum*, and which is variouſly modified with regard to its firmneſs and denſity, according to the diffe-rent modes of its extraction, and peculiarities of the parts from whence it is taken.

It is evidently compoſed of two parts very dif-ferent from each other, and which prevailing or diminiſhing, either in their ſeparate or joint capa-city are capable of affecting the moſt important revolutions in the animal œconomy.

Many have been the attempts made, in order to eſtimate the proportionate quantity of the craſ-ſamentum to that of the ſerum in human blood

when

when drawn from its containing veffels, yet are we not able from any experiments hitherto made, to eftablifh a *certain* conclufion.

Their *apparent* proportions are very fallacious ; being confiderably varied by thofe circumftances which influence the time neceffary to effect its concretion, and from the time of its coagulation to that of its proportions being examined.

We have had numerous opportunities of ob-ferving the influence and effects of collateral cir-cumftances in blood letting, and could never ac-curately determine the proportionate quantities of the red cruor and ferum.

We have frequently been able to join the learn-ed Haller in affirming that, " In maffa fanguinea " media pars, et ultra, cruoris eft. In robore " valido ferum minuitur ad tertiam partem, in " febre ad quartam et quintam reducitur, in mor-" bis a debilitate increfcit* ;" and as often have

* Vide Primæ Lineæ, parag. 137.

we

we found the ferum abundant, and the craffamentum reduced to a third or even fourth part.—But
even fuppofing we were in poffeffion of the moft
exact eftimate of the ferum with refpect to the red
cruor, yet muft it ftill remain undetermined what
proportion, the red globules and gluten (of which
the red cruor is compofed) bear to one another,
and confequently, it is not fully afcertained what is
the ufual proportion of red globules in the blood
of perfons in a ftate of health.

It feems highly probable that in a healthful
ftate of the body, not only the red globules, but
alfo the gluten may be increafed or diminifhed, in
proportion to the *quantity*, or in fome meafure according to the *quality*, of the aliments taken in
during a given time : but this will not fully ena-
ble us to determine what is the proportion in the
healthful bodies of different perfons, and confequently what fhare they may afford in giving a
difference of temperament.

N

In

It may be prefumed however, that with refpect to the ferofity, the proportion of red globules and of gluten taken together, will be greater or lefs according to the digeftive and affimilating powers in each perfon ; and that thefe again will be according to the general ftrength or weaknefs of the fyftem*.

We have already faid that the red cruor is compofed of two feparate and diftinct parts, but firft let us examine it as an aggregate body, and which is fpecifically heavier than the ferum, by about *one twelfth* part.

By the heat of a water bath it affords an infipid water, and then becomes dry and brittle. It gives over by diftillation an alkaline phlegm, a thick, fœtid, empyreumatic oil, and volatile alkali in a confiderable proportion.

* Vide Cullen's Materia Medica. Chap. I, Sect. I. Page 69.

The refidual coal is porous, and of a brilliant and metallic afpect, very difficult of incineration, affording vitriols of iron and of foda, when united with vitriolic acid in a certain degree of heat, leaving a mixture of carbonaceous matter and cal- careous phofphate.

It readily putrifies when expofed to a warm air, and is feparable into two diftinct fubftances, by maceration in water, which becomes tinged more or lefs with a red colour, by one of the fubftances which it holds in folution; and this mixture when heated with different menftrua, exhibits all the characteriftic properties of *ferum*, differing prin- cipally in the greater quantity of iron it contains, which is very confiderable, and may be obtained by incineration of the refidual coal, and afterwards iviating, in order to feparate the faline particles.

This metal it naturally contains in the ftate of calx, and which is eafily reducible by the addition of any oleaginous, or carbonaceous matter, with the

the affiftance of heat, as we have already had occafion to remark in a former part of this work.

The refidue after lixiviation is faffron of Mars,
of a beautiful colour, and moftly attracted by the
magnet. It is to this metal that many have attributed the colour of the blood.

The red globules we have already defcribed,
and fhall therefore proceed to an examination of
the coagulable lymph, which is the third and
laft component part of the blood.

It is this fubftance, which being diffufed
through the other part of the blood, takes a concrete form when expofed to the influence of air ;
or when difcharged from its containing veffels
into any part of the body ; and which being
thrown out upon furfaces may produce adhefions
of parts, which in their natural ftate were not u-
nited, but in fome cafes admitted of free motion,
many inftances of which we have in the lungs adhering

hering to the ribs, pericardium to the heart, &c. and in anchylofis where it is poured round the joints in a fluid form, manifeftly filling up the chinks of bones, and intervals of futures ; and which being thrown out upon wounds is the moft natural balfam both for the defence and union of the divided parts*.

The coagulation formed by this ftubftance becoming at length organized, veffels may be clearly feen ramifying through it ; as in moles or falfe conceptions which in general are nothing more than coagulated blood, which had been gradually collected at different times from the veffels of the uterus, and are difcharged at a particular time, and have frequently been found wholly vafcular. Thefe, however, have been known to take their rife from a retention of the embryon placenta, which fometimes remains after the expulfion of the gelatinous fætus in the early months, the

* Vide note to page 44 and 45.

bulk of which is encreafed by additional coagula, and its confiftence may probably be rendered more denfe by abforption of the more fluid parts ; when excluded in this ftate it has been called a *falfe conception*. But if it fhould remain longer, and acquire the confiftence of a fchirrus, having loft all traces of its ever having been an organic body, it is called a mola. This mola or mole is generally expelled in the courfe of the fecond, third, or fourth month, if it fhould continue longer, it may prove extremely troublefome by the flooding it occafions ; and, in weakly delicate habits, may induce death*.

There are however inftances in which thefe mola have remained in the uterus for a very confiderable time, without producing any material injury, and even the entire fætus has been known to have been retained in the uterus or abdomen for years ;

* Vide La Motte, Mauriceau, Smellie, Hamilton and other practical authors on Midwifery.

fome-

fometimes during a long courfe of life. A very remarkable inftance of which I remember to have occured at the Village of Ilkefton, near Notting-ham: the woman fometime after conception re-ceived a kick on the gravid uterus, foon after which, labour pains came on, but again went off, without effecting the delivery of the child,—fhe lived upwards of forty years after this accident without experiencing much inconvenience from the prefence of the child, which was evidently felt during the whole of that long term. On in-fpection after death, the uterus was found lacer-rated towards the right fide, and the whole of the fœtus (except the head) was found in the cavity of the abdomen where it had formed numerous adhefions with the contained vifcera ; having be-come organized by the ramification of veffels very evident and numerous throughout the whole. At the time of this infpection it exhibited figns of be-ginning putrefaction.

The coagulable lymph is in fhort the general

bond

bond of union between parts that were feparated. By it are broken bones, and wounded parts u- nited, and afterwards become organized, as is proved by the phenomena of the growing callous, exuding in minute drops from the inmoft fub- ftance of the bone and not from the periofteum as fome have imagined; and which in procefs of time gradually indurates.

This *gluten* may be extracted from bones by a chemical analyfis; it contains grofs earthly par- ticles, and may be diftinguifhed by the juice of madder, the colouring matter of which ftrongly adheres to it.

The *lymph* not only changes from the natural ftate to the more watery, but fometimes varies from the natural to the more vifcid and coagula- ble, producing thofe inflammatory crufts which are found in fome difeafes covering the different parts of the body.

Thus

Thus we have many inftances, where the out-fide of the heart, and infide of the pericardium have been found covered with a cruft equally tough as the fize ufually found in pleuritic blood, the furface underneath having marks of inflammation but no ulcer.

Probably therefore this change may be produced by inflammation, or by exciting the exhalant arteries to fecrete a lymph, with fuch an encreafed difpofition to coagulate ; and this fuppofition is rendered probable, from a cruft having fometimes been found on the inner furface of the heart, fimilar to that we fo often obferve formed on its outer furface ; a peculiar inftance of which was obferved by Sir John Pringle in a perfon who died apopleftic, having previoufly laboured for fome time under a palpitation of the heart; on infpeftion of the heart, there was found evident marks of inflammation on its furface, and an abfcefs on the right ventricle, which muft inevitably have burft, had not an opening from it been co-

O   vered

vered and fhut up by a fmall cruft or polypus, which occupied a fpace in the ventricle.

Now as the flow of blood through the heart is ftrong and conftant, had not the lymph forming that cruft, coagulated inftantly on being fecreted it muft have been wafhed off by the blood, and as the coagulable lymph is not naturally difpofed to fo inftantaneous a coagulation, it is more than probable that a morbid affection of the veffels endued them with the power of effecting this change ; as by an increafed heat and action either of the whole fyftem, or of particular parts.

The fluids which moiften the different cavities of the thorax, abdomen, &c. are very probably compofed of a mixture of this lymph and water, and that mixture varies from the dropfical, where the aqueous parts are confiderably more abundant, up to the rheumatic or inflammatory habit where the lymph abounds and the watery parts are pro-portionately diminifhed ; and numerous obfervations

vations confirm, that in fome cafes the lymph in
paffing through inflamed veffels, is converted into
the ftate of a purulent matter, fimilar to that
which is found in well conditioned ulcers, &c.

Hence it is obvious, many and various diforders
may derive their origin, from particular modifications of the quantities and confiftence of this
fluid. And hence a powerful argument in favour
of the opinion, that pus is fometimes fecreted in
its perfeft ftate from the mafs of blood: for
if we allow that the exhalant veffels fecrete, at one
time an aqueous fluid, at another gelatinous lymph,
and at a third, when fomewhat inflamed, that
lymph fo vifcid and fo much altered in its properties as to coagulate inftantly on being fecreted,
it is equally probable that they may fometimes,
when more inflamed, have the power of fecreting
that lymph in the form of pus. Mr. Hewfon
in one inftance found three pints of pure pus
in the pericardium, without any ulcer of that
membrane, or of the heart. And in another the

cavity

cavity of the pleura of the right fide was fo much diftended with pus as to comprefs the lungs into a very fmall compafs, and which partook more of a whey-like fmell than of a putrid fluid, but without any appearance of ulcer or erofion, either on thefe organs or on the pleura, there being only a thin cruft of coagulated lymph under the pus.

There are fome furfaces of the blood which are defended from the influence of the external air by mucus, but we find under circumftances of imflammation that coagulable lymph is thrown out upon them, and which by infpiffation forms a membranous appearance; an occurrence which often takes place in the courfe of the alimentary canal. Mr. Cline remarked a cafe of this kind in a boy who had fuch a membrane throughout the whole length of the inteftines.

Confumptive perfons have been fuppofed to fpit or cough up their lungs, when it was nothing elfe than the coagulable lymph, which had been

adher-

adhering to the bronchiæ, and which muft have greatly obftructed refpiration ; after thefe are dif-charged, the complaint vanifhes, and the patient is eafy until more is formed.

Another particular phenomenon which is, exhi-bited by the coagulable lymph and which very much directs practitioners in judging of the pre-fence of inflammation, is fuppofed to arife from any inflammatory affection exifting in any part of the body, as the lungs, or any of the vifcera, &c. and frequently found on the furface of coagulated blood, and which hath been denominated the *buff* or *fize*. This appearance is produced by a por-tion of the gluten feparating from the craffamen-tum and is much firmer in texture than this laft, upon the furface of which it is found.

Sydenham obferves " That if you agitate the " veffel while the blood is coagulating, this ap-" pearance does not take place ;" he therefore concludes " that it depends more on accidental circumftances

" cumftances than on any morbid change, as the
" manner in which the blood is drawn from the
" body &c. He remarks, that if it be fuffered to
" trickle down the arm, no fuch phenomenon fu-
" pervenes, but that if drawn in a full ftream the
" inflammatory cruft feparates from the mafs ;".
however we do not always find this to be the cafe;
we ought not therefore from the abfence of fuch
appearance, to conclude againft the prefence of
inflammation; fince a variety of circumftances in
blood-letting may prevent this feparation of gluten from taking place in blood otherwife difpofed to it*.

When the blood after cooling and concreting,
fhews a portion of the gluten feparated from the
mafs, and laying on the furface of the craffamentum; as fuch feparation generally occurs in all
cafes of more evident phlegmafia ; fo in ambi-
guous cafes, we from this appearance joined

* Vide Cullens firft lines.

with

with other fymptoms, infer the prefence of inflammation.

It would feem that the formation of this buff
in fome meafure impeded the coagulation of the
blood, for Mr. Cline remarked, that in a patient who laboured under an acute rheumatifm,
his blood did not coagulate in *twenty four hours*,
nor then till he removed the inflammatory buff
from the furface, and I have frequently obferved
that fuch blood as afforded this fize in the greateft
quantity, was proportionately longer in coagulating, and in two inftances where the patients had
been much exhaufted by previous blood-lettings,
the blood afforded nothing elfe than a portion of
this fize fwimming upon the furface of a large
quantity of ferum, of a dark tawny hue, which
being kept for fome days, advanced to putrefaction without any further feparation.

The circumftance of its being longer in coagulating led Mr. Hey to imagine that it was owing to
the

the ferum being diffufed through the craffamentum.

It is a curious circumftance that blood taken in
different cups from the fame perfon and at the
fame time, will differ very confiderably in the
proportion of this fize. Mr. Hewfon thought and
with great probability that it was owing to the
manner in which the veffels are acting at the
time when the different portions are drawn off;
for the action of the veffels is encreafed by inflammation, and as the action of the veffels de-
creafes, the fizy appearance becomes proportionably lefs. If twelve ounces of blood is taken in
three cups, the firft will have little or no appearance of buff, the fecond a good deal, and the
third lefs.

That the firft has no fize upon it, may be owing to the apprehenfions of the patient ; fear being known evidently to diminifh the action of the
veffels, fometimes occafioning fyncope, and even
death.

death. That this depends in a great meafure on the action of the arteries may be further proved by bleeding an animal to death; and in operations it has been a frequent obfervation, that the blood coagulates fooner in proportion as the patient becomes faint.

Size will fometimes appear when there exifts no real inflammation, but only an increafed action of the arteries, as is evident from the blood of pregnant women; which if drawn in a full ftream and fuffered to ftand till it coagulates, always exhibits an appearance of buff upon its furface: but when the quantity is confiderable we may reafonably infer that the blood has fome inflammatory tendency.

This gluten was confidered by many phyficians as a preternatural and morbid matter, but we now very certainly know, from many incontefti-ble proofs, that it is conftantly a conftituent part of the human blood, and that it is produced folely

P   by

by a peculiar feparation of the parts of the blood,
effected in confequence of inflammation and fome
other circumftances, giving rife to the appearance
which was erroneoufly confidered as a mark of
a morbid lentor in the blood. That fuch a preternatural lentor does ever prevail in the general
mafs of blood, we have no direct proofs of; the
experiments of Dr. Browne Langrifh on this fubject, afford no conclufion, having been made on
certain parts of the blood feparated from the reft,
without attending to the different circumftances of
blood-letting, which we have already remarked
have great influence on its feparation and concretion.

It is well known that all the animal fluids, but
efpecially the gluten, is inclined to putrefaction;
and that even in the living body if frefh aliments
be not very conftantly taken in : and that alfo if
certain excretions which carry off noxious or putrefcent matter, be not duly fupported, a confiderable tendency to putrefaction takes place.

Hence

Hence Dr. Cullen fuppofes that fome degree of putrefaction exifts very continually, even in the moft healthy ftate of the animal ; and that it appears moft evident in an evolution of faline matter, which being taken up by the aqueous parts conftantly prefent, forms the ferofity, and that the ferum which is obtained by fpontaneous feparation, confifts of a portion of gluten diffolved in this faline fluid*.

It would appear, from the name of *ductus aquofi* given to the lymphatic veffels, that their firft dif-coverers fuppofed the lymph to be mere water.

This opinion was rendered more probable by fome of the fucceeding phyfiologifts, and particu-larly by the learned Boerhaave, who fuppofed that there were three feries of arteries : the *fanguiferous*, carrying true red blood, the *feriferous*, carrying the ferous parts without the red globules, and the

* Vide Cullen's Inftitutions of Medicine.

lymphatic,

lymphatic, which had each their correspondi ng veins destined to restore their particular fluids to the heart.

Thence the lymph seems to have been conclud_ ed the thinnest part of our fluids; which opinion was confirmed to physiologists by Leuwenhoeck's theory, that the globules of lymph were smaller than either those of the serum, or of the red parts of the blood.

The fluids that moisten the different cavities of the body, as of the peritoneum, pleura, pericar- dium, &c. having been suspected to be formed solely from the condensation of that steam which issues from the opening of animals just killed, have thence been considered as mere water by se. veral anatomists and physiologists, who imagined their opinions confirmed, by observing, that in dropsies, where a large quantity of fluid is dis. charged from such cavities, it is generally mere water, very rarely coagulable by exposure to air,

or

or the influence of heat; and agreeably to this opinion they fuppofed, the fluids, fupplied by nature for the moiftening of thefe cavities muft be the fame as thofe evacuated from them in dropfical cafes.

But however plaufible the arguments from which fuch conclufions were drawn, it appears from experiment, that notwithftanding their tranf-parency in living animals, and their being fo *watery* in cafes of dropfy, yet in the healthy ftate of animals they differ fo effentially from pure water as not only to coagulate when expofed to heat, but alfo by mere expofure to air; and in this circum-ftance they are perfectly analogous to the coagula-ble part of the blood called the *coagulable* lymph ; as is evidently demonftrated by collecting this fluid from the furfaces of the abdomen, thorax, peri-cardium, &c. of an animal that has been recently killed, while in a ftate of health ; for if the fluid thus collected be fuffered to reft, it will take a

concrete

concrete form, as the coagulable lymph of the blood does, by expofure to air.

This is an experiment which Mr. Hewfon made on a very confiderable number of animals, as on bullocks, dogs, geefe, and rabbits; nor did the refult of any of the experiments differ.

From among thofe who concluded thefe fluids to be a mere water, fhould be excepted Drs. Haller and Monro, who are of a different opinion.

If immediately after killing an animal in health, a lymphatic veffel be properly fecured by ligatures, fo as to prevent the efcape of its contents, and then cut out of the body and opened, fo as to let out the lymph into a cup or other veffel, and expofe it to the air, it will become gelatinous, as the coagulable lymph of the blood would do, under fimilar circumftances. This experiment Mr. Hewfon has alfo made feveral times, and we

have

have frequently repeated them with fimilar refults, on dogs, affes, and geefe.

Since then thofe fluids in healthy animals coagulate fpontaneoufly on expofure to air, may we not conclude that they are the fame as the coagulable lymph of the blood, at leaft they would feem more efpecially of that nature, than either the water, or the ferum, which latter do not coagulate on being expofed to the air? and it would appear an argument much in favour of this inference, that fuch a fluid feems better adapted to the purpofe of lubrication than *mere water*, and more perfectly analogous to the *fynovia*, which of all fluids is the beft fitted for that purpofe?

Although from thefe, and other experiments of a like nature it would feem fufficiently evident, that the lymph in the different cavities and veffels of an healthy animal, will always coagulate on expofure to the air, yet it is equally certain that the confiftence of that coagulum will vary in different

ferent

ferent animals, and even in the fame animal according to the different circumftances of health ;
nor will the differences of time required for their
concretion be lefs obvious ; inftance, thefe fluids
in *geefe* will coagulate fooner than thofe in dogs.

Mr. Hewfon remarks that in moft of the dogs
which he examined, the lymphatic fluids formed
a ftrong jelly ; but in a dog which he had fed
eight days with bread and water only, and that
too fomewhat fparingly, this jelly was but very
weak.

That age has fome influence on the concretion
of thefe fluids, would feem fully confirmed by
obferving that in young animals, as geefe, &c. the
coagulation does not take place fo foon as in fuch
as are full grown, nor is this obfervation lefs juft
with refpect to the fluid contained in the pericardium and abdomen of other animals ; which fluid
when in a fmall quantity, perhaps *always*, forms a
ftrong jelly ; while on the contrary if it be in a
                                    confiderable

confiderable quantity, and the animal in a feeble
or debilitated ftate, it will be found proportionably thinner.

In dropfical cafes, the fluid evacuated from
thefe cavities, has, I believe, very rarely been
obferved to coagulate on expofure to air, as the
fluids natural to thofe cavities would do in a perfectly healthy ftate of the animal.

In fome cafes it has been found capable of
coagulating by heat, like the ferum of the blood,
while in others it has undergone no further alteration than that of becoming flightly turbid though
boiled for a confiderable length of time.

Though we have faid it rarely happens, that
thefe fluids, collected in any very confiderable
quantity, and through the influence of difeafe, are
capable of coagulation, by expofure to air, or
without the application of heat, yet do we not
mean to infer, that this can *never* take place; on

Q

the

the contrary we *have* feen, more than once, the fluid evacuated from an *afcites* by the operation of tapping, acquire by reft in a moderate temperature, a truly gelatinous confiftence, though in but a *flight* degree, as might naturally be expected from the large quantity of water in proportion to the coagulable matter.

We have alfo frequently obferved, when examining the bodies of fuch as have died labouring under dropfical affections, that a confiderable portion of perfectly gelatinous matter has been feparated from the fluid contained in the abdomen; in a manner very fimilar to the fpontaneous feparation which takes place in the blood when effufed from its proper veffels; and not feldom have we found the fluid naturally contained in the pericardium converted into a concrete tremulous jelly.

Although this lymph is more abundantly aqueous in a debilitated ftate of the animal, yet

is

is it lefs watery and more coagulable in fome difeafes.

But a ftill more curious fact, is, that in thofe cafes where the fluid contained in the pericardium and abdomen of animals in different ftates of health, has been compared with that of their lymphatic veffels they, were uniformly found to agree with regard to the confiftence and degree of coherence of the jelly which they formed.

For when the animal was in perfect health, the lymph from the cavity of the pericardium, abdomen, and pleura, formed a ftrong jelly, and that in the lymphatics of the neck and extremities was equally firm.

When the animal was reduced, as in the dog, fed *eight days* on bread and water only, or when the goofe was very young, the coagulum formed by the fluid contained in the cavities of the perecardium, &c. was very weak, and that of the lymphatic veffels, in the fame proportion. Hence, although

though thefe fluids may be fubject to variations according to the different circumftances of health, yet do they feem always to agree with each other.

What would feem to confirm our idea with refpect to the lymph contained in the lymphatic veffels, approaching very nearly and with very flight difference, to the nature and properties of the coagulable lymph of the blood, is their peculiar property of taking a concrete form by expofure to air, although the former differs from the latter in the time neceffary for their coagulation.

In dogs of apparent perfect health, whofe blood and lymph were difcharged from their containing veffels at the fame time, the latter was found to require a much longer time for the procefs of coagulation than the former.

The time which the blood generally requires to perfect its coagulation feldom exceeds *ten minutes*,

* Vide p. 49.

but

but the fluid evacuated from the lymphatic veffels was found to require upwards of *half an hour* for the completion of that procefs.

And although in weak animals the coagulation of the blood is more expeditious, yet the contents of the lymphatic veffels, or the fluids contained in the cavities of the pericardium, &c. feem lefs in-clined to coagulate in proportion as the animal is reduced, or the fluids become more watery.

The principal differences which are obferved between the contents of the lymphatic veffels, and the coagulable lymph of the blood, feem to arife from the difference of time required for their co-agulation, either when expofed to the air, or when confined from its influence, and merely fuffered to reft in their proper veffels ; in the latter cafe however they moft evidently differ.

In a dog, killed whilft in apparent health, and whofe *veins* and *lymphatic veffels* were fecured by

ligature

ligature immediately after death, the blood in the
veins was completely coagulated in the courfe of
fix hours, whilft the lymph of the *lymphatic veffels*
remained perfectly fluid, even at the expiration of
twenty hours after death ; yet on expofure to air
for fome time it acquired a gelatinous confiftence.

We have already remarked that the ferum of
the blood only, forms good pus ; but that in certain cafes the cavity of the pericardium, &c.* has
been found to contain a confiderable quantity of
pus, without any appearance of ulcer or erofion.

Hence in thefe cafes as pus is produced merely
by fecretion, may we not with great probability allow, that even in abfceffes, where there is a confiderable lofs of fubftance, the pus is not formed
fiom a diffolution, or melting down of the *folids*,

* Vide p. 107.

but

but being fecreted into the cellular membrane, &c. from its preffure, or other caufes, deftroys the texture of the folids and then diffolves them. This feems to be ftrongly confirmed by an experiment which we have frequently repeated and uniformly with the fame refult ; to wit, having put a piece of frefh meat, into an ulcer, and covered it up, its texture was foon deftroyed, at the fame time rendering the pus more fœtid.

And this opinion of pus, being in fome inftances at leaft formed by fecretion, feems more evidently confirmed by obferving that in its pure ftate it is full of *globules*, in which circumftance it bears a refemblance to milk, which is produced by fecretion, and not by fermentation.

From what we have faid then, it would appear that the lymph contained in the lymphatic veffels, and the fluids which moiften the different cavities of the body, as the pericardium, pleura, peritoneum, &c. far from being *mere* water, are in

healthy

healthy animals coagulable fluids, very nearly approaching to the nature of the coagulable lymph of the blood, and of which at least it is highly probable they may be a species, perhaps compofed of that very lymph in a state of dilution with water; and that the different proportions of the mixture vary from the dropfical habit, where the coagulable lymph is in fmall, and the aqueous parts in great quantity, up to the highly inflammatory habit, where this lymph abounds, and the water is in lefs proportion; and that even in fome inftances the lymph, by paffing through inflamed veffels, has been converted into pus.

There is yet another part of the blood, which deferves our attention perhaps not lefs than any of the former.

It is that *fibrous matter*, called by Malpighi and Gaubius the *fibra fanguinis*, by Senac the *coagulable lymph*, and by Dr. Cullen the *gluten of the blood*; which when feparated fpontaneoufly from
the

the reſt of the maſs, and laying on the ſurface of the blood drawn out of the veſſels of living ani-mals, conſtitutes a principal part of that membra-nous appearance known to phyſiologiſts under the denomination of the inflammatory cruſt, concern-ing which we have already delivered our ſenti-ments*.

This fibrous matter is generated in great abun-dance from the *craſſamentum*, but from the ſerum in ſmaller quantities. They may be obtained by putting the blood into a linen cloth, and lixiviat-

---

* Leſt it ſhould be underſtood by what we have advanced with regard to this phenomenon, in a former part of this treatiſe, that the *coagulable lymph* (properly ſo called) was alone inſtrumental in the production of this inflammatory cruſt; we beg leave to obſerve, that it is by its union with the *fibrous matter* that it becomes adapted to that purpoſe; and that perhaps in almoſt every inſtance this fibrous mat-ter is abſolutely neceſſary to its formation. At leaſt there can be no doubt of this, in caſes where the cruſt has ac-quired any conſiderable degree of tenacity.

ing

ing with a confiderable quantity of water, until it runs through perfectly clear.

The refiduum after this ablution feems chiefly to confift of a white, fibrous matter, equal in quantity to about the *twenty eighth* part of the whole mafs.

Thefe fibres, having been wafhed, according to the above mentioned procefs are perfectly white, colourlefs, and infipid. They are formed from the coagulable lymph but are not generated in the courfe of circulation, fince in blood recently drawn from the living animal, and before it has begun to coagulate, thefe are not to be perceived by the microfcope, which fo eafily renders vifible the moft minute red globules: nor does their long thread like figure feem adapted for receiving motion.

By diftillation on the water bath, they give over an infipid phlegm, of a faint fmell, and which readily putrifies. This fibrous matter hardens in

a

a fingular manner by expofure to the moft gentle heat; and when fuddenly prefented to a ftronger heat, it fhrinks up like parchment.

It affords by diftillation in a retort, an alkaline phlegm, a ponderous, thick oil of an abominable foetid fmell, and a confiderable quantity of ammoniacal chalk contaminated with oil; the refidual matter is a denfe, heavy coal, of no great bulk, and much more eafy of incineration than that of the lymph; the afhes are perfectly white, apparently earthy, feeming to confift chiefly of phofphate, and do not contain the fmalleft portion either of faline matter or of iron, being deprived of both thefe fubftances by the previous lixiviation.

Thefe fibres advance rapidly and with great facility to putrefaction; when fubjected to the influence of a hot and moift air, they fmell, and afford volatile alkali in confiderable proportion. It is totally infoluble in water, and when expofed

to

to a boiling heat in that fluid, it indurates and assumes a greyish colour. Alkalies are incapable of effecting its solution; but the most feeble acids combine with it.

Mr. Berthollet has observed, that in its union with nitrous acid, a considerable quantity of mephitis is disengaged, and afterwards nitrous gaz, the solution being accompanied with effervescence; when this gaz is set at liberty, oily and saline flocks may be observed floating in the residuum, which is a yellowish fluid; this liquor by evaporation affords crystals, analogous to the acid of sugar or oxaline acid, and deposits a very considerable quantity of flocks formed of a peculiar oil and calcareous phosphate.

The fibrous part of the blood seems to contain two oils, one, which with the oxegynous principle, constitutes the oxaline acid, the other with the same principle forming the malusian acid. The muriatic acid dissolves the fibrous

mat-

matter, forming therewith a greenish jelly. It is dissoluble in vinegar by the assistance of heat. It is precipitated from the acid solution by alkalies, and even water, no longer exhibiting the same properties, after being separated from these acid menstrua; being decomposed in combination with those solvents.

It is not altered by the admixture of neutral salts, or other mineral substances. It readily combines with lymph, than which it is a more perfectly animalized substance. This animal gluten greatly resembles that of flour, but it possesses in a much more eminent degree the remarkable property of becoming concrete by cooling and rest.

It will appear evident from what has been advanced, that this matter is of the utmost importance in the animal œconomy and that many very useful facts of no inconsiderable consequence in practice may be derived from a more scrutinous atten--

attention to this fubftance than hath hitherto been
paid by phyfiological or pathological writers.

It has been long fince obferved that, it is
formed from a difpofition of its original matter
in the mufcles, conftituting the fibrous bafe of
thofe organs, and compofing that fubftance
which is moft eminently irritable. Hence it may
be infered that it is capable by its abundance or
deviation, of giving rife to many and peculiar
diforders*.

By the foregoing obfervations on the fibrous
matter we have fhewn it to confift principally of
a gelatinous gluten, and a certain terreftrial fubftance.

Thefe elementary particles begin to cohere,
even while the fluids are in *ovo*, and foon acquire

* Vide a memoir of M. de Fourcroy's in the volume of
the Royal Society of medicine for 1783.

their

their fibrous or thread-like appearance. And on the different proportions of the terreftrial and gelatinous matter neceffary to the formation of the fimple fibre depends the various degrees of hard-nefs and foftnefs in the different parts of the body ; and from the firm cohefion of thefe parts, or the defect therein, Boerhaave deduces the gene-ral fource of difeafes*.

Although it is not our intention here to treat of difeafes with their feveral caufes, and the modes of cure ; yet would it not feem irrelavant that we fhould make fome curfory remarks on that ftate of the body induced by a laxity of the animal fi-bre called by Dr. Fordyce the general weak-nefs.

He obferves that this may be divided into two kinds. The firft in which both fenfibility and irritability are encreafed : the fecond in which

---

* Vide Boerhaave's aph, and Haller's Element: Phy-fiolog. on the animal fibre.

thefe

thefe fenfations are confiderably diminifhed ; as in apoplexy and palfy.

The *firſt* is called fingle weaknefs, and may again be fubdivided into two varieties ; firſt, when by any means it is fuddenly produced, and in which cafe it is in general eafily reſtored.

Secondly, when it comes on flowly, and in which cafe it is with difficulty reſtored.

Hence thefe two differ effentially ; both as to their caufes, fymptoms, effects upon the fyſtem, and the mode of cure. The fecond is called a paralytic weaknefs.

Weaknefs may be induced by various means, thus, bleeding, all evacuations when too copious, and continued for too great a length of time, by leffening or exhauſting the living power, produce this effect.

A

A particular part may be weakened by exciting a fecretion from the mucous gland of that, or
contiguous parts, though not connected with it.

The fyftem may be ftrengthened by various
means, firft, by *nourifhing* and *ftrengthening* diet,
which if the veffels have been fuddenly emptied,
fhould be adminiftered freely, for the veffels are
capable of receiving as much as the power of the
conftitution can eafily digeft ; and by this means
the ftrength is foon reftored. If the difeafe has
come in a more flow and gradual manner, the influence of good nutritious food will not be fo
fpeedily exerted ; for any confiderable debility
of the organs of digeftion, brought on gradually,
renders the procefs, of digeftion by far more
difficult and flow ; in fuch cafes proper food,
exhibited in moderate quantities, and frequently
repeated, has often proved extremely beneficial.

The arteries fometimes, have a confiderably increafed action in hectic fevers : thence it becomes

necef-

neceffary fometimes to diminifh the degree of contraction, by blood-letting ; and then the patient
may be capable of receiving nourifhing diet, not
only without inconvenience, but even with manifeft advantage.

When the ftomach is in a weak ftate we fhould
cautioufly avoid thofe vegetables that produce
acidity in the primæ viæ ; hence cabbage, beans,
peas, &c. are by no means proper ; but the farinaceous feeds, properly prepared and given in
conjunction with animal food, are beft.

Secondly, the body may be ftrengthened by
exercife. When exercife is ufed it fhould not
be to excefs, but fhould be equal and univerfal
through the whole body, and not in any one part
more than another ; and on this account, riding
in a carriage, &c. is much preferable to any
other, as the motion of the body is more equal ;
but in cafes where more violent exercife is required,
riding on horfeback will be of great fervice.

Exer-

Exercife fhould always be taken in as free and pure air as poffible; for thus the circulation is increafed and becomes more free, paffing through the lungs without any obftruction; whereas in a moift air the lungs are always more or lefs obftructed, and anxiety, &c. is produced.

It is perhaps equally neceffary, in moft inftances, that the kind of exercife fhould be pleafing or agreeable to the patient—that the mind may be open to pleafureable affections.

Thirdly, the ftrength may be encreafed, or reftored by means of cold, which contracts the extreme veffels, and hence the more internal ones about the precordia, are kept filled, which tends very confiderably to the prefervation of ftrength.

It moreover diminifhes the irritability of the fyftem, and prevents people from fo readily fuffering by expofure to cold.

If

If the cold be very fuddenly applied, it contracts the extreme veffels in too great a degree, by which the more interior ones become overloaded, and febrile difeafes, &c. fupervene. Hence expofure to cold fhould be gradual, that is, it fhould be by living very continually in a cold atmofphere, yet fhould it not be too confiderable, though applied flowly, for its powers of exhauftion are capable of producing weaknefs, numbnefs of the limbs, anxiety, &c. this however depends upon the degree of cold to which the animal has been habituated. But in no cafe fhould the tranfition from heat to cold, or from cold to heat be fudden.

The *cold bath* has been ufed for the purpofe of ftrengthening the fyftem, but it would feem a very uncertain remedy; for as we have already re-marked a very fudden expofure to cold contracts the extreme veffels too much, keeping the more interior ones filled, fo that after the patient comes out, the heart acts with greater force and propels

it

it again upon the skin, producing fweat; and by this a kind of paroxyfm is brought on.

It is no doubt in fome cafes of very confiderable fervice; but in difeafes attended with debility, and where there are confiderable fecretions, as in gonorrhea benigna, &c. the difcharges are fometimes reproduced, inftead of being taken off.

A temperate bath, in which is diffolved a quantity of aftringent ftubftances as fea water, &c. acts as an aftringent on the skin after the patient comes out, and frequently ftrengthens the fyftem.

Cold climates have a much greater tendency to ftrengthen the habit, than the warmer ones, as in the former the denfity of the atmofphere, renders refpiration more falutary and free.

Fourthly, the fyftem may be ftrengthened, by the patient being fituated fo as to breath properly,

and

and infpire fuch air, and in fuch quantity as is neceffary for the welfare of the animal œconomy.

There are two effects of confiderable importance produced by refpiration on the blood ; firft, by propelling it through the lungs, fo as to prevent its accumulation in the right fide of the heart ; and in the fecond place, by what it imparts to, and receives from the blood, its colour is changed from a dark to a more florid red*.

The want of *pure air* induces anxiety, &c. which is foon followed by weaknefs ; thofe who live in large and populous cities or towns, are infinitely more fubjected to difeafes arifing from debility, than thofe who live in the country or villages thin-ly inhabited ; in which latter they are generally more robuft, and fubject rather to inflammatory complaints ; notwithftanding a cool air generally

* We have already fpoke fomewhat largely on this fubject, and to which we muft refer the reader.

con-

conduces to the increafe of ftrength, when the patient is exhaufted by profufe evacuations, yet by
fending them into the country the purer air there
may too much accelerate the circulation ; and as
the large veffels at this time contain but a fmall
quantity of blood, fuch a degree of weaknefs may
be brought on as to eventually deftroy the patient.

Medicines are the next means of reftoring
ftrength. Thefe are fuch as invigorate the folid, principally by encreafing the living power ;
of this fort are camomile, gentian, wormwood,
peruvian bark, and fome other of the vegetable
bitters.

Various mineral productions are frequently
found ufeful in reftoring the tone of the fyftem ;
among the metals *iron* is found to be peculiarly
adapted to this purpofe.

All thefe diminifh irritability at the fame time
that they give tone to the relaxed fibres.

In

In thofe cafes where the fyftem hath been very fuddenly weakened, but not fo much fo as to impair either the appetite or organs of digeftion, a nou-rifhing diet will often fuffice, without the admi-niftration of thofe remedies. If, for inftance, a patient is much reduced by a fever, and fome flight inflammatory fymptoms remain, it is better to omit thefe medicines ; but if any confiderable degree of fever is ftill prefent, with want of appe-tite, colliquative purges, &c. and the ftrength does not return, we may ufe them with advan-tage ; and if debility be fuddenly induced, at-tended with partial evacuations they may be ef-pecially ferviceable, and perhaps none more fo than the *peruvian bark.*

When weaknefs is gradually brought on, thefe medicines may be employed with very confider-able advantage, if fuitable precautions are not neglected.

Firft, in melancholic temperaments where there

is

is eventually a contraction of the veffels, as well as a weaknefs, indicated by a hard pulfe; but before we employ them it would be neceffary to take off this difpofition to contraction by evacuations. However it frequently happens that in melancholic habits, we cannot by any means employ them.

2. They are apt to lofe their influence on the fyftem, by ufe; for if you adminifter them for a certain length of time, their effects will at firft be fully produced, and the patient feem to be very much relieved, but their effects will foon diminifh by continuance, until they are, in a manner, loft; for this reafon it is perhaps better to vary the medicine; giving the bark and fteel altetnately, and occafionally leaving them off for a time, fo as to prevent their becoming habitual to the patient, who after a fmall time, again repeating them, will derive confiderably more benefit from their ufe, andhis ftrength will more fpeedily be reftored.

When debility fupervenes flowly, and in con-

T   fequence

fequence of lingering difeafes, it is in general better
to exhibit other bitters and ftrengtheners than the
bark.

In moft cafes when the moving powers are in a
lax and debilitated ftate, preparations of iron are
preferable to either the bark or bitters; but where
a ftimulus is wanting to the fyftem, they can be
of little fervice.

Iron may be exhibited with moft advantage in
a ftate of folution, we fhould however remember,
that ferruginous preparations are feldom admif-
fible in melancholic habits, fince their ftimulant
or aftringent powers are apt to produce coftivenefs.

We fhould always cautioufly avoid giving tonic
medicines for this difeafe in too large dofes, other-
ways they will only tend to aggravate the complaint*.

* Vide Edenb. Med. Com Vol 4, p. 339—413.

Having

Having taken notice of the difeafe arifing from a laxity of the *fibre*, it may not be lefs important to add fome curfory obfervations on the phenomena of irritability in which the fibrous parts are a very principal inftrument; and although there have been many abettors of the opinion, with regard to the fibres of the perioftium, tendons, and ligaments being devoid of fenfibility*, yet we now very certainly know that the phenomena of inflammation render manifeft the irritability and fenfibility of parts, which in an healthy ftate did not feem to be in poffeffion either of the one or the other.

Many and various have been the opinions of phyfiologifts on this fubject†. The three noted claffes of animal powers, *elafticity*, *irritability*, and *fenfibility*, have been and are yet too much confounded, although it is no difficult task to diftin-

* See the works of Drs. Haller and Hunter, De Hean, &c.

† Vide Haller, Whytt, De Hean, Kirkland, Cullen and others.

guifh

guifh thefe affections of the fibres from one a-
nother.

The force and nature of elafticity, poffeffed by
the fibres, which, only in degrees, prevades all
parts without exception, was fully known to Bel-
lini, Baglivi, Stahl, Pacchioni, Juncker, &c.
This power known to Stahl's followers under
the appellation of tone, has no fimilarity to irritability, fenfibility and vital powers, fo called;
it does however, either alone perform the action of the animal and vegetable body, or adds
ftrength and vigour to them ; the former is manifeft in the motion of the ribs and cartilages, and
the latter in the conftriction of the uterus, veffels,
and membranes.

It is by no means fubject to the laws of life
only, but may continue even for a confiderable
time after death ; nor is it completely deftroyed
but by putrefaction alone. It may during life
be diminifhed by various caufes, and again be reftored by feveral remedies.

Irri-

Irritability, which Haller thought exifted in the fibres of the mufcles alone, in name indeed but not in reality, and which was known to Gliffon, is a new genus of animal power; nor does the word *enormoun* of Hippocrates fignify the fame thing. It would feem almoft proved by the experiments of Lups, Haller, Fontana, Hoffman, and feveral others, that it is different from elafticity in its rife, duration, feat, caufes, effects, and phenomena. Wrisberg remarks, firft, that it is moft powerful in the mufcular fibres of the whole body but not equally difperfed through all ; more powerful in the heart, mufcles of refpiration, and inteftines ; becomes gradually weaker among the voluntary mufcles, and perhaps, remains but in a trivial degree in the veffels, and membranes; but however fome always exifts, as appears from the doubts offered by Whyt, De Hean, Van Doeveren, &c. which have been anfwered by Haller, and the learned Cigna.

Secondly, the phenomena of irritability and

irre-

irritation, themfelves, by which thofe are produced, do not always agree ; for in fome it advances in a regular tract, fo that from the flighteft
irritation you will always obferve a manifeft irritability ; This is nearly the cafe in all the mufcles.

In many other parts you may obferve, the
greateft inconftancy, and irregularity of effect ;
being one thing to day, another to-morrow ; now
encreafed, now diminifhed, at one time yield to,
at another refift, the irritating power : all which
is evident in the skin, vifcera, veffels, and iris.

Thirdly, the learned pathologifts Eller, Tiffot,
Gerhard, have long ago acknowledged the very
great rife of the doctrine of irritability. It would
be of great importance to be well acquainted with
the remedies, whether they be medicines, or remedies from diet, or otherwife, which particularly
conduce to excite irritability, if it is languid, or to
diminifh it if it is too great.

Opium

Opium and the other narcotics, camphor, cantharides, acrid poifons, bark, and the electric fpack, fhew a clear influx of animal fpirits in the production of irritability.

Fourthly, That it is different from the faculty of feeling, and therefore by no means dependent on the *nerves*, appears from the irritability of vegetables, and from other reafons. The faculty of feeling, depending folely upon the nerves, although it has been regarded as one and the fame thing with irritability, has been more ftrongly oppofed by Haller's opponents, De Haen, Whytt, Le Cat, Gerhard, &c. than irritability itfelf. But according to Haller's and Caftell's experiments, that fenfibility of parts is to be refined both to the various quantity of the nerves, their fituation and condition, and to the various violence of irritation, and nature of the irritating or offending body, fo that they may be at times more or lefs painful ; and at other, as Haller thinks, they may be altogether infenfible.

We

We shall not repeat what has often been ob-
jected to, that a greater pain having preceded,
abforbs, or blunts a lefs pain following ; as we are
not fenfible to the tafte of a drop of wine having
taken a very fmall quantity of rectified alcohol
upon the tongue a little before.

It cannot however be denied, that in inflammatory
difeafes, affections of the mind, and other caufes,
it may happen that hurt parts may now feel, which
under any other condition might feem to be
infenfible.

The *vital power* of certain learned, and more
modern authors, as Vanden Bos, Bikker, Gau-
buis, Albinus, &c. feems rather to be compounded of all the animal powers comprehended together : which opinion except in fome minutiæ,
the great Boerhaave and Simpfon have more exactly adapted*.

* Vide Profeffor Wrifberg's notes on Haller's Element·
Phyfiolog.

Per-

Perhaps no theory has ever been advanced on the laws of irritability equal to that of the learned Girtanner, whofe memoir on the laws of irritability, &c. is fo elegantly tranflated in Dr. Beddoe's obfervations, that we fhall give an abftract from it *verbatim.*

" The irritable fibre, he fays, from the firft moment of its exiftence to that of its defolution, being conftantly furrounded by the body which acts upon it, and ftimulates it, and upon which it re-acts by its contraction, it follows, that during the period of its exiftence the irritable fibre is in continual action ; that its exiftence confifts in action ; and that it is not a paffive ftate as fome authors have afferted.

" Hence, external objects having no immediate action upon the nerves, and only acting upon them, and producing their different fenfations through the medium of the irritable fibre, it is plain that the ideas we have of external objects are not

U   conform-

conformable to thofe objects, but that they are varied and modified by the irritable fibre through which they are tranfmitted to us.

" Objects therefore appear different according to the different ftates of the fibres: The irritable fibres which are combined together in every individual, whether animal or vegetable form a fyftem of fibres, in which the integral parts act continually upon the whole, while the whole reacts upon the parts, fo that every ftimulus which acts upon any fibre in the fyftem will deprive it of part of its irritability; but this lofs will foon be repaired by the fyftem, and every fibre will furnifh in proportion, fome fhare of its own irritability to fupply the lofs in any one fibre. Thus it is that a very weak ftimulus, but one that is conftantly acting upon one part of the fyftem, fuch as flow poifons, the abufe of fpiritous liquors, &c. exhaufts in the end the whole fyftem, and produces death.

" For

" For the fame reafon a very powerful ftimulus applied to one part of the fyftem, fuch as laurel water, opium, the poifon of the rattlefnake, will in an inftant exhauft all the irritability of the fyftem, deftroy the animal, and leave the fibres without any irritability.

" I am convinced, fays he, from repeated experiments, that opium, alcohol, ammoniac, a folution of fugar of lead, fulphuric æther, deftroy animals by exhaufting the irritability of the whole fyftem, and that the mufcles of the animals deftroyed, have, by application of thefe ftimuli, been wholly deprived of their irritability*.

* Dr. Beddoes remarks, and we would think very juftly, that it is incredible that many poffitive ftimuli, fuch, for inftance as the vegetable poifons of the tropical countries; and the venom of certain ferpents, which produce death in quantities fo aftonifhingly minute, fhould, as Dr. Girtanner imagines exhauft the irritable principle, by combining with it directly themfelves; nor could alcohol, opium, and oil of lauro cerafus, be fuppofed to attract from the irritable fibre, (if we confider only the quantity in which they produce their

" The

" The effect was the fame when thefe ftimuli, were applied to the mufcles and ftomach, and when injected into the veins of animals.

" The irritable fibres in the fame fyftem have not all the fame degree of irritability, they have different degrees of *capacity* for the irritable principle. The capacity of the fibres is in the ratio of their diftance from the heart. Thofe equally diftant have the fame capacity. Every ftimuli which affects one of the fibres affects the others at the fame time and in the like manner.

" Hence the fympathy of different and feparate parts, and thofe furprifing phenomena which hitherto have been explained by the harmony of the nerves, although we fee the fame phenomena in the vegetable kingdom, which is deprived of nerves.

effects,) a large quantity of oxygene. But fuppofes it more likely that they occafion a *new combination* of oxygene, throughout the whole fyftem.

" Thefe

" Thefe fympathetic phenomena are obfervable throughout organized nature. Whatever part of the polypus be touched the whole will contract ; and its arms will contract themfelves by fympathy. If a worm be touched with the point of a pin, without wounding it, the whole worm will be feen to contract itfelf ; which is a certain proof that the different parts are affected by fympathy.

" If the flighteft impreffion be made on one of the leaves of the averrhoa carambola, not only that leaf but all the neighbouring ones will con- tract themfelves by fympathy.

" When the irritable fibre has loft its tone, and fails, either from an accefs of the irritable princi- ple, or from a deficiency of this principle, it is difeafed and the fyftem of which it forms a part fuffers and becomes difeafed, through fympathy. All the difeafes of animals may be ranged under two heads ; to wit ; firft, the *difeafes of accumulation* caufed by the accumulation of the irritable prin-

ciple

ciple and the diminifhed action of the habitual ftimuli.

" Secondly, the *difeafes of exhauftion* caufed by a defect of the irritable principle proceeding from the encreafed action of the habitual ftimuli, or from the addition of new ftimuli. Under thefe two claffes may be ranged all difeafes whatfoever.

" Paradoxical as this propofition muft neceffarily appear to thofe who have not reflected on the fubject, it is neverthelefs true, and I fhall give the moft convincing proofs of it in a work I am about to publifh."

" Remedies remove the difeafe by their action upon the irritable fibre, and by exhaufting its irritability, when the difeafe is that of accumulation or by diminifhing the action of the common ftimuli and confequently by preventing a total exhauftion, where the difeafe is that of exhauftion.

The

The effects of poifons are to be explained in this way.

" Poifons, remedies, and in general all furround-ing bodies acting only on the irritable fibre, it fol-lows that they act upon the fyftem in a fimilar manner, and that every fubftance capable of pro-ducing the greateft poffible effect upon the fibre, that is to fay, every fubftance capable of exhauft-ing all the irritability both of the fibre itfelf and of the fyftem in an inftant ; as for inftance, laurel water, or white arfenic, is alfo capable of produc-ing all the inferior degrees of action, either by acting upon a fibre lefs irritable, or by acting upon the fame fibre, but in a lefs quantity.

" Laurel water, opium, white arfenic, ammo-niac, are of courfe both medicines and poifon, ca-pable of healing as well as of producing all ma-ladies whatfoever without exception.

This

" This truth feems to be of the utmoft importance; and the Abbè Fontana, who made more
than fix hundred experiments to prove that ammoniac is no remedy againft the bite of a viper,
would have faved himfelf a great deal of trouble,
had he been acquainted with it*.

" If inftead of applying the venom of the viper
to fo many animals, and afterwards applying ammoniac to the wound, he had made a fingle comparative experiment, and had applied ammoniac
to a wound made by a lancet that was not poifoned, he would have found that ammoniac itfelf,
applied in this manner, would have produced a

* What muft be the flate of medicine when the truth of
this theory is eftablifhed?—The ftudy of the fcience will then
only in general be profecuted through motives of curiofity,
and a defire of knowledge, the practical part being necefla-
rily confined to fuch narrow limits, as to occupy the time and
attention of but a comparatively, very fmall number of pro-
feffional men.—That, that period may arrive, is a confum-
mation devoutly to be wifhed.

difeafe

difeafe exactly analogous to that caufed by the venom of the viper, and, confequently fo far from
removing the malady, muft neceffarily increafe it
by exhaufting the irritability of the fibre in a
much lefs time, than the venom of the viper, by
itfelf, was capable of doing.

"Mr. Fontana has made upwards of fix thoufand experiments upon the poifon of the viper ;
he employed more than three thoufand vipers, and
caufed to be bit more than four thoufand animals,
and the conclufion he drew after this truly enor-
mous number of obfervations was, that the poifon
of the viper kills all animals, and produces the
difeafe by its action on the blood.

"But why did Fontana neglect to make the decifive experiment, the *Experimentum Crucis* of Bacon ?
It is well known that frogs, and many animals
with cold blood, live a long time without the
heart and entirely deprived of blood. If therefore the poifon of the viper kills animals by its

X   action

action on the blood, it would not deftroy frogs without blood. But experiment contradicts this reafoning. The poifon of the viper will kill frogs without blood in as fhort a time as it kills thofe animals that have not loft their blood.

" It is not therefore by its action on the *blood* that the venom of the viper deftroys animals ; and thus does it happen that a fingle experiment frequently overturns all that fix thoufand other experiments have apparently eftablifhed.

Dr. Girtanner concludes from his own experiments, that poifons operate upon the blood juft as they do upon the mufcular fibre, by depriving it of its principle of irritability, or of its oxygene.

" The effect produced upon the irritable fibre by any ftimulus, is in a ratio compounded of the degree of irritability of the fibre, and of the force of the ftimulus. The fame ftimulus will produce

greater

greater contractions upon a fibre more irritable, than upon one lefs irritable; and the irritability of the fibre being the fame, it will contract itfelf more upon the application of a ftronger than of a weaker ftimulus.

" The effect produced upon an irritable fibre by any ftimulus is in the inverfe ratio of the repetition of its application. Cæteris paribus, the effect of any ftimulus diminifhes every time its application is repeated, till at laft the effect is nothing, or $= 0$.

" This explains the phenomena of habit, and many other phenomena hitherto inexplicable in the animal and vegetable œconomy. The mimofa pudica, for example, expofed to a ftrong wind, contracts itfelf; but it ceafes to contract itfelf in obedience to this ftimulus after it has been accuftomed to it.

The

" The effect produced upon the irritable fibre
by any ftimulus, is in a ratio compounded of the
degree of irritability of the fibre, and the degree
of the force of the ftimulus directly, and the degree of the habit of the fibre, inverfely. Let
the force or intenfity of the ftimulus $= a$, the
degree of irritability of the fibre $= b$, the degree
of the habit of the fibre $= c$, then the effect produced upon the fibre or x will $= \frac{a\,b}{c}$. But all the
ftimuli acting in the fame manner, that which
diminifhes the irritability of the fibre for a certain
ftimulus, will in like manner diminifh it for the
ftimulating force in general, wherefore the habit
of the fibre is comprehended under its degree of
irritability, or c is comprehended under b. Therefore x will $= a\,b$.

" The effect produced upon the irritable fibre
by any ftimulus or x being always equal to $a\,b$, it
follows that the value of a and b being known, the
value of x is alfo known. But admitting an uni-
ty fixed and conftant, it will be eafy, in all cafes,

to

to exprefs by numbers, the degree of irritability of the fibre, and the degree of the force of the ftimulus, or the value of *a* and *b*, confequently it will be eafy to find the value of *x*.

" All the art of medicine then confifts in finding the value of *x*, that is to fay, in finding a ftimulus adequate to reftore the tone of the fibre.

" Thus, if thefe principles be true, phyfic, which at prefent is an art of mere conjecture, will be reduced in time to the certainty of calculation, and after tables fhall be formed to exprefs the valves of *a* and *b*, and the figns by which they may be known, this calculation will be fo fimple and eafy, that it will form a part of the education of every individual. But further, the irritable fibre being the fame in all organized nature, difeafes and their remedies will of courfe be the fame for all organized beings; there will then be no diftinction between medicine, farriery, and agriculture, but all thefe fciences will be confounded and become

one

one, under the general name of *univerſal phyſio-logy.*

Theſe ſtimuli which I call common and habitual, becauſe they act continually more or leſs upon the irritable fibre, are, *heat, light, nouriſh-ment, air, the circulation of the blood, the ſtimulus of generation,* and *the nervous ſtimuli.*

So long as the action of theſe ſtimuli is in proportion to the degree of irritability of the ſyſtem, and the ſum of their action is nearly equal to the ſum of the irritable principle abſorbed by the lungs and diſtributed by the circulation, the whole ſyſtem will be in proper order, and the conſtituting fibres will have their tone.

When one or more of theſe ſtimuli act more powerfully than ordinary, or the fibre becomes more irritable, while the degree of the action of the ſtimuli remains the ſame, the *exhauſtion* of the

ſyſtem

fyftem, and one of the difeafes in its train, will be the confequence.

The abfence of one or more of thefe ftimuli, will produce an *accumulation* of irritability in the fyftem, and give birth to one of the difeafes of this clafs. I fhall fpeak of thefe ftimuli, feparately, in order that I may be better able to explain my-felf.

Of heat—The heat of the atmofphere and of all furrounding Bodies, acts upon the fibre and ftimulates it. I am convinced of the ftimulating action of heat from direct experiments. I have expofed fmall animals, fuch as cats, dogs, rabbits, &c. in covered veffels, to the heat of boiling water, which furrounded the veffel in which the animal was placed, fo that the water could not touch it. Animals deftroyed by heat in thefe experiments, upon diffection, have been found to have loft all their irritability. Their heart and mufcles contracted themfelves but feebly, even upon the

appli-

application of the ftrongeft ftimuli, fuch as electricity.

It is proved, by fome beautiful experiments of
Mr. Hope, that heat acts as a ftimulus upon plants;
and it is obfervable that plants expofed to the fun
are larger and produce more flowers and fruit
than thofe which are lefs expofed to heat. Trees
in general are more luxuriant which grow in the
fouth than thofe in the north. This is a proof
that heat is a ftimulus to the irritable fibre.

The difeafes of hot climates are all the difeafes
of exhauftion, caufed by the two powerful action
of the ftimulus of heat. Hence the cuftom of taking ice in hot countries to reftore the tone to the
fibre, by abforbing the heat and preventing its
ftimulating action.

The irritability of the hedyfarum gyrans is exhaufted by the heat of the noon day fun, according to the obfervations of M. Brouffonnet; and

by

by the experiments of M. Fontana, and M. Medicus it is proved that, the the irritability of plants is great in the morning, dimifhed during the heat of the day, and little or none in the evening.

Of cold—" Cold being of a lefs degree of heat, its effects upon the irritable fibre are in proportion to the habit, or the quantity which is neceffary to the fibre to preferve its tone. The animals and plants of hot climates, that require the ftimulus of a great heat to preferve the tone of their lefs irritable fibres, are affected by the leaft obftruction of this habitual ftimulus ; the irritability of their fibres accumulates in confequence of their obftruction, the return of the heat again exhaufts the fibre. The more intenfe the cold is, the greater is the accumulation of irritability. After the fibre has been expofed for fome time to a great degree of cold, its irritability is encreafed to fuch a degree, that the moft trifling degree of heat produces the moft violent effects : hence the glow experienced after coming out of a cold bath ; hence

the

the difeafes which are caught in coming out o
the cold air into a warm room, and which medical men attribute to checked prefpiration, a fuppofition entirely falfe.

" The leaft movement is attended with fatigue
upon the fummit of high mountains, as I have
frequently experienced, but efpecially in 1785, upon the top of the *Buet*, and as M. Sauffure has
likewife obferved, upon the fummit of *Mount
Blanc**. The reafon of it is this, the fibre is

* " Les forces mufculaires s'epuifent avec une extrême
" promtitude.---Ce qui diftingue & caraƐterife le genre de fa-
" tigue que l'on eprouve á ces grandes hauteurs, c'eft un
" epuifement total, une impuiffance abfolue de continuer fa
" marche---On ne feroit pas á la lettre quatre pas de plus,
" fût-ce pour eviter le danger le plus eminent.—Si l'on per-
" fifte a faire des efforts, on eft faifi par des palpitations &
" par des battemens fi rapides & fi forts, dans toutes les arte-
" res, qui l'on tomberoit en defaillance ; fi on l'augmentoit
" encore in continuant de monter.

" La feule ceffation de monvement, dans trois ou quatre
ren-

rendered fo irritable by the cold of thofe Mountains, that the leaft motion of the mufcles, or
what is the fame thing, the leaft action of the nervous ftimuli, exhaufts it. It is by the gradual application only of heat that frozen limbs can be
recovered, and it is neceffary always to begin by
rubbing them with fnow ; without this the fibre
will be exhaufted, and become gangrenous.

" minutes, femble reftaurer fi parfaitement les forces, qu'en
" fe remettant en marche, on eft perfuadé qu'on montera
" tout d'une haleine jufques à la cime de la montange. Or dans
" la plaine une fatigue auffi grande ne fe diffipe point avec
" une telle facilité. Mr Piétet fe trouve toujours faifi d'une ef-
" pece d'angoiffe, d'un leger mal de cœur, & d'un degout
" abfolu, defqu 'il eft arrivé a la hauteur d'environ 1400
" toifes au deffus de la mer." (Vide Sauffure Voyages, 4to.
I. 482, &c.)

Mr. Sauffure likewife tells us that on the Col de Géant, at
1763 toifes above the level of the fea, " Le charbon ne brû-
" loit que d'une maniere languiffante, & a force d'être
" animé par le foufflet." (*Journ. de Phys.* Sept. 2788, p. 209.

" During

" During the winter, by the abfence of the ſtimulus of heat, and in part of light, plants and many animals become torpid, the organs of circulation and of nutrition perform their funĉtions but
languidly, and life itſelf appears ſuſpended. In
conſequence of the diminiſhed aĉtion of theſe ſtimuli, the irritability accumulates, and manifeſts
itſelf at the return of ſpring. The leaſt degree of
heat then produces the moſt violent effeĉts upon
the fibres thus delicately irritable.

" Animals, which. had concealed themſelves
under ground, venture forth from their ſubterra-
neous retreats, plants put forth their leaves and
flowers, and man himſelf is ſenſible of the ſtimulus
of heat in the gales of ſpring ; his fibre being
rendered more irritable by the winter's cold. Vegetation is much more vigorous in ſpring-time
than during the reſt of the year. It diminiſhes
during ſummer in proportion as the irritability
accumulated during winter is diminiſhed by the
action

action of heat and light, and laftly, is exhaufted in the autumn.

" Dr. Hales obferves, that the rapidity with which the fap circulates in the vine during fpring is five times greater than the rapidity with which the blood flows in the arteries of a horfe.

"This motion is much flower in fummer, and almoft ceafes in autumn. It is not the effect of the heat alone, for if that were the cafe it would increafe as the heat increafed, and the effect would be proportionate to the caufe; it is the effect of the irritability accumulated in confequence of the abfence of heat during the winter. The effects of winter are very great in cold climates, becaufe the accumulation of the irritability is in proportion to the abftraction of the ftimulus of heat. In Lapland corn ripens in fixty days, whereas in France it requires an hundred and twenty or an hundred and thirty days.

" The

" The truth of what I have advanced may be proved by expofing vegetables alternately to heat and cold : it is furprifing how much their growth and the power of vegetation is increafed. But in thefe experiments care muft be taken to vary the temperature by degrees ; becaufe the irritability accumulating in the fibre by the abftraction of heat, a very fmall quantity of this ftimulus then applied is fufficient to exhauft it entirely, or to deftroy it. Hence it is that the return of cold and froft in the beginning of fpring is fo noxious to vegetables, and that the year is in general more abundant after a very cold winter.

" Mr. Fontana obferved, that during the winter the vipers which he kept for his experiments were in a torpid ftate, though the thermometer was at 59°. He endeavoured to render them vigorous by warmth and expofed them to a heat of 67° only. In two minutes they died, though during fummer they bore a much greater degree of heat ; but then they are lefs irritable. *Spallanzini*

obferved

obferved that *newts* bury themfelves in the earth and become torpid in the month of October, before the thermometer in the fhade falls to $54°\frac{1}{2}$, and that they re-appear in the month of February, though at that time it freezes every night, and frequently during the day, and the thermometer is many degrees below $54°$. What is the reafon, enquires this excellent obferver, that thefe animals revive in fpring, when the cold is more intenfe, and fink into torpidity at a much lefs degree of cold in autumn ? I will folve this problem by obferving that in autumn a very great ftimulus is required to act upon the fibre of thefe animals, exhaufted as it has been by the heat of the fummer ; but in fpring, the leaft ftimulus, the leaft increafe of heat is fufficient to put the fibre in action, its irritability having accumulated during winter, in confequence of the abfence of the common ftimuli.

" *Light* is another common ftimulus. To convince myfelf of the ftimulating quality of light upon

upon plants by direct experiments, I enveloped
the leaves of some plants in an opaque body, so
that the air might have free accefs, while the light
could not penetrate. I found that thefe leaves
became more irritable than the others, the irritability having accumulated. By the abftraction
of the ftimulus of light, the irritability of organized bodies accumulates, and a difeafe enfues,
which is called *etoilement.* Animals deprived of
light, and living in dark places, lofe their colour,
and become white, as obferved in arctic animals
during the long nights in the countries near the
pole : I have obferved it alfo in animals that inhabit the Alps, and which conceal themfelves for
the greateft part of the year in fubterraneous
dwellings. *Blanched* plants lofe their green colour
and become whitifh and fickly. Some poifonous
plants lofe their noxious qualities and become a-
greeable to the tafte, merely by the abftraction of
the ftimulus of light. White animals and plants
are very irritable ; and it is obferved that thefe
animals

animals and plants are not capable of fupporting a great quantity of light.

" The action of the light upon plants has been very well obferved by Dr. Ingenhoufz and Mr. Senebier, and the manner in which colours are produced has been explained by M. De la Methe-rie. It is well known that animals that have been tamed, and efpecially domeſtic animals, change their colour by education; but an obfervation that has perhaps efcaped naturaliſts is, that this change is conſtantly from dull colours to thofe that are brighter or lefs dull. I have often ob-ferved that the change takes place more frequent-ly in dark than in light places. Mice kept in a cage in a dark room have produced white mice."

" The third common ſtimulus *is that of nutri-ment.* It requires a very fmall quantity to fupply the daily loffes; the greateſt portion is employed in depriving the ſtomach, and of courfe the whole fyſtem, of its fuperfluous irritability. This is

Z

proved

proved by what is obferved in organized bodies.
All animals are more irritable before than after
food.   Hunger, of which appetite is the leaft degree, is caufed by the accumulated irritability of
the fyftem."

" The *gaftric juice* acts upon the fibres of the
ftomach become more irritable, and produces
the fenfation of hunger. Spallanzani has obferved
that birds of prey do not void indigeftible bodies,
fuch as pieces of glafs or metal, which they have
taken in with their food, before their ftomach is
empty.

" Thefe indigeftible bodies cannot be voided
while the ftimulus of the nutriment acts upon the
ftomach; but as the abftraction of this ftimulus
gives the irritability of the ftomach an opportunity of accumulating, the indigeftible bodies very
ftrongly ftimulate the fibres of the ftomach, make
them contract, and by this contraction they are
voided. It is poffible to do almoft wholly without

out nutriment, by applying, from time to time, fome other ftimulus to the ftomach, fuch as tea, coffee, alcohol, opium, and by thefe means exhaufting the accumulated irritability of that organ.

" By the entire abftraction of the ftimulus of nutriment, the irritability of the fyftem is prodigioufly increafed. There are many inftances of perfons, who, not having eaten any thing for many days, have been intoxicated and killed in confequence of fwallowing with greedinefs, two or three cups of broth.

" Plants fuddenly tranfplanted from a meagre, into a rich foil, produce no fruits or feeds, and die in a fhort time of a particular difeafe, caufed by excefs of nutriment.

" The *circulation of the fluids* is the moft powerful of the common ftimuli. The blood which oxygenates itfelf during its paffage through the
lungs

lungs, parts with its oxygene in the circulation, the oxygene having a ftronger attraction for the irritable fibre than for the carbon which is con-tained in the blood.

" In this operation the heat combined with the oxygene is fet free, hence animal and vegetable heat. The blood acts continually upon the irri-table fibre, and the fibre re-acts upon the blood, and this action and re-action are ftronger in pro-portion as the circulation is more rapid, and as the air which comes in contact with the blood in the lungs contains more oxygene air.

" When any local ftimulus continues to act upon any part of the fyftem, the circulation be-comes more rapid, and a fever is the confe-quence.

" Is the ftimulus weak, a flow fever enfues, which will by little and little exhauft the irritabi-lity of the fyftem, and the patient will die of a
con-

confumption. Is the ftimulus ftronger, or the fibre upon which it acts more irritable, we fhall have an ardent fever, which will exhauft the irritability in a lefs time.

" In fine, is the ftimulus very violent, or the fibre difeafed by an excefs of irritability, we fhall have a putrid fever, which will deftroy the patient, whether animal or vegetable, and will exhauft the irritability in a very fhort time.

" But whatever be the nature of the fever, the fibre irritated by the ftimulus will act upon the blood more than ordinarily, the re-action of the blood will be increafed in proportion, the circulation will be more rapid, the blood will abforb more oxygene, and the whole fyftem will be furcharged.

" By this means the irritability will be increafed, the animal heat augmented, and the effect of the action of the ftimulus becoming greater, in
proportion

proportion to the accumulation of irritability, a total exhauftion of the irritability, or the death of the patient, will enfue.

" There are two methods of prevenring the fatal effects of a local ftimulus, whofe operation upon one part of the fyftem is conftant. The firft confifts in preventing the furcharge of oxygene in the blood, which is accomplifhed by diminifhing the proportion of oxygene gaz in the air breathed by the patient, or by diminifhing the quantity of blood by phlebotomy. The fecond method confifts in applying ftimuli capable of exhaufting the irritability in proportion as it accumulates; fuch as wine, opium, bark, heat, &c. Phlebotomy acts by diminifhing the quantity of blood, and confequently its operation is attended with this effect, viz. of diminifhing the re-action, and reftoring to the fibre its tone.

" I fhall here obferve by the way, that the advice which many phyficians have given, to make

the

the patient breathe oxygene gaz, is the moſt per-
nicious they can give; for the patient always
finds himſelf worſe after having breathed this
oxygene gaz, as I have frequently had occaſion to
obſerve."

" The *nervous ſtimulus* is the only one which is
peculiar to animals.   It is this ſtimulus which is
the cauſe of the voluntary motions, of convul-
ſions, and paſſions.   The paſſions differ from one
another only in ſtimulating the irritable fibre
more or leſs.   Anger and joy are very powerful
degrees of the nervous ſtimulus; content and
hope are weak degrees; fear, ſorrow, fright,
deſpair, are not abſolute degrees of this ſtimulus,
they are only the abſtraction of the ſtimuli of
hope, content and happineſs.

" Anger and joy act as very powerful ſtimuli
and exhauſt the irritability of the fibre in the ſame
manner as any other ſtimulus whatever.   Content
                                                            and

and hope are degrees of the nervous ſtimulus, neceſſary to preſerve the tone of the fibre.

" Sorrow and fright are degrees too weak. If they continue to act, the irritability of the fibre accumulates. It is well known that fearful and melancholy perſons are oftener affected by the ſtimulus of contagious diſeaſes than they who are free from fear, and who take the precaution of applying a greater quantity of ſtimulus than ordinary to their fibres, by taking wine, vinegar, opium and bark.

" According to the obſervations of Mr. Fontana, timid and fearful animals die much ſooner of the bite of the viper than courageous or irritated animals.

" Joy, excited by the annunciation of good news, to a ſorrowful perſon, and one of courſe very irrible, has often cauſed death. The ſtory of the Roman Mother is well known, who was bewailing the
death

death of her fon, and who dropped down dead for joy, the moment fhe faw him enter her room alive.

" By the abftraction of many of the common ftimuli for any length of time, the irritability of the fibres accumulates fo much, that the moft trifling ftimulus produces the moft violent effects, and frequently even inftantaneous death.

" This difeafe is called the fcurvy, concerning the nature of which medical men have formed fo many falfe and ridiculous theories. It is of the utmoft importance to mankind to know the true nature of this difeafe; fince, in confequence of our ignorance in this particular, we have been unable to find a fure remedy for it, and fo many thoufands of lives have fallen a facrifice to its ravages, in armies, fleets, and befieged towns.

" In the laft war, the Englifh fleet fuffered dreadfully from the fcurvy; and laft year many

2 A   fol-

foldiers died of this difeafe in the imperial city in
Walachia, in confequence of the abftraction of the
ftimulus of nutriment, (the Emperor having or-
dered that a kind of pafte, made of bread and
water fhould be given to the foldiers inftead of
meat) of the ftimulus of oxygene, in the corrupt-
ed atmofphere of the fens of Walachia, and laftly of the nervous ftimulus, the moft powerful of
all ; for the greateft part of the army were engaged by force and againft their inclinations.

" The abftraction of all thefe ftimuli accumulated the irritability of the fibre, and caufed the
fcurvy, and that dreadful mortality that took
place in the army. The fame caufes produce the
fame effects on other animals. We fee domeftic
animals affected with the fcurvy in confequence of
cold and hunger, that is to fay, in confequence of
the abftraction of the ftimuli of heat and nutriment.

" The fheep which Captain Cook had on
board his fhip, on his voyage round the world, in
the

the years 1772, 3 and 4, died of the scurvy, their
teeth fell out, their gums rotted; in a word, they
had all the symptoms of an inveterate scurvy.
The abstraction of the common stimuli in plants
produced similar symptoms and a similar disease.

" The disease of Rye called *ergot* is exactly analogous to the scurvy in animals* ; the *ergot* is the
scurvy of plants; it is the effect of accumulated
irritability in the fibres of plants. The causes
which produce the scurvy in animals, according to the observations of *Saillant* and *Tessier*,
are, a wet and barren soil, and a cold sum-
mer ; that is to say, the causes of the *ergot*
are, the abstraction of the stimuli, of nutriment
and heat.

---

* See Dr. Trotter's very valuable Treatise on this disease,
Edit, 1792---Beddoes' Observations, &c. where not only all
the symptoms, causes and effects of this disease are fully explained, but also an almost infallible remedy is pointed out ;
known to modern chemists under the denomination of the
citric acid.

I

" I could enlarge upon this interesting subject, if I were not afraid of making this essay too long. I wished to give only the outlines, or a general view of my theory, without entering into the detail. In the subsequent essays I shall treat of oxygene considered as the principle of irritability, or the composition or decomposition of water in animals and plants, of the different kinds of air contained in the interior cavities of organized bodies, and of the circulation of this air, the existence of which has not hitherto been even supposed, although, as I shall prove hereafter, the lymphatics in animals, and the fibres in plants, are almost solely destined for the circulation of these elastic fluids ! ! ! "

Such are the general outlines of a new system of physiology founded by the ingenious Dr. Gir tanner, and from which we may at least derive many very important facts.

Having endeavoured to prove that the principle of life was dependent on irritability, or rather

that

that irritabily is itfelf the principle of life; he proceeds to examine the principle of irritability, and to prove that oxygene is itfelf that principle; which is conveyed to the blood in the lungs by the function of refpiration and thence diftributed to every part of the fyftem in the courfe of circulation; combining with ftimulating ftubftances, which come in contact with different parts of the fyftem.

He is decidedly of opinion that *oxygene* is abforbed by the blood, and that the *venous blood,* is oxygenated in the lungs during refpiration; whereas the moft celebrated naturalifts, phyfiologifts and chemifts are of a directly oppofite opinion, fuppofing that oxygene does not combine with the venous blood; but that the latter lofes *carbon* and *hydrogene* recovering the florid colours natural to it, without the affiftance of any principle abforbed from the atmofphere, and from the following experiments have they drawn their conclufions.

Firft, by expofure to hydrogene air *arterial blood,*

becomes

becomes deprived of its vermilion colour, affuming the black and darker hue of *venous* blood; while a part of the hydrogene air becomes abforbed.

Secondly, Mr. Hamilton made three ligatures on the jugular vein of a cat; and having expelled the blood from between two of the ligatures, he introduced the hydrogene air and kept it there, clofing the aperture through which it had been introduced. He then loofened the middle ligature, and the blood contained between that and the third ligature came in contact with the *hydrogene air*, and about an hour afterwards, having taken the blood from the vein, he found it liquid, and of a dark colour, nearly approaching to that of ink.

Thirdly, *Venous blood* by expofure to *vital air*, acquires the bright vermilion colour of *arterial blood*, rendering the air impure.

The

The following conclusions have been drawn from these experiments by Mr. Lavoisier and Dr. Crawford*.

First, That the change of colour, which the blood undergoes, during the course of circulation, is produced from its combination with *hydrogene air*.

Secondly, That in its passage through the lungs, the blood gives out a portion of the hydrogene it contains, and then resumes its vermilion colour.

The above mentioned authors suppose that during respiration the vital air which is received into the lungs, combines with carbon and hydrogene disengaged from the blood ; forming *carbonic air* with carbon, and with hydrogene *water*, while the blood, having lost the carbon and hydrogene

* Vide Annales de Chimie, tom. 5. p. 267—Crawford on Animal Heat.

with

with which it had been charged during its circulation, again recovers its vermilion colour.

We may however, without detracting from the merit of thofe highly diftinguifhed philofophers, very readily infer, that thefe conclufions do not *neceſſarily* refult from thofe experiments, and we now very certainly know that they are to be explained in a manner more conformable to the laws eftablifhed by modern chemiftry.

We know of no experiment which might authorize us to fuppofe that carbon can unite with oxygene in a temperature of 97°.—99°, or that hydrogene and oxygene airs combine and form water in fo low a temperature.

M. Seguin has attempted to anfwer this objection, by fuppofing that the carbon is in a very attenuated ftate in the blood, and by citing the experiments of Mr. Bertholet upon hydrogene air.

But

But this explanation appears hypothetical, and no way convincing.

Having for a confiderable length of time paid very particular attention to the phenomena of refpiration, and after having made numerous experiments upon this fubject : Dr. Girtanner concludes, that during refpiration one part of the oxygene of vital air combines with the *venous blood*, changing its black colour to that of a bright vermilion ; and which the ingenious Dr. Goodwin has long fince proved*; the fecond part of this oxygene unites with the carbon contained in the carbonic-hydrogene gaz, which exhales from the venous blood, and forms carbonic acid air ; a third part is combined with the carbon of the mucus, which the lungs contain in great quantities, and which is in a continual ftate of decompofition ; forming alfo carbonic acid air ; and a fourth part of this

* Vide Goodwin's Conne&tion of Life with Refpiration p. 61.

oxy-

oxygene combines with the hydrogene of the blood to form water, which is exhaled during refpiration.

That portion of heat which was contained in the vital air previous to its decompofition, now remains united in part with the oxygene and the blood.

Hence the peculiar difference of heat in *arterial* and *venous* blood.

Another portion of heat enters into combination with the carbonic acid air, and a third part produces a temperature neceffary for the formation of water, by the combination of the hydrogene and oxygene airs.

Hence the effects of refpiration will of courfe be thefe.

Firft,

Firft, That the venous blood becomes deprived of the carbonic hydrogene air which it contains, and abforbs oxygene air, which gives rife to its vermilion colour, which it likewife imparts to metallic oxids, nitrous acids, and feveral other fubftances with which it enters into combination.

Secondly, As oxygene increafes the capacity of all fubftances with which it unites, fo will the capacity of the blood be encreafed.

Thirdly, The oxygene air of the atmofphere is in part abforbed by the venous blood, partly changed into carbonic acid air by the carbon of the blood and the mucus of the lungs, while the remainder in combination with the hydrogene air forms wa-ter, and a quantity of heat is fet at liberty. Con-fequently the products of refpiration will be—

1. Animal oxid, fluid (i. e. arterial blood.)

2. Carbonic acid air.

3. Water.

4. A fmall quantity of liberated heat.

From

From this theory it cannot be difficult to explain the experiments we have cited.

If we expofe arterial blood to the contact of hydrogene air, the quantity of air will be diminifhed, lofe its vermilion colour, and become livid.

In this experiment the exact reverfe takes place of what is obfervable in refpiration. The hydrogene air combines with the oxygene air of the blood to form water, while the *arterial blood* thus deprived of its oxygene becomes black, and having the appearance of venous blood; affuming a deep colour only from the want of oxygene.

Mr. Hamilton's experiment proves this, he alfo adds that he found the blood liquid and very little coagulable. The Doctor obferves in his firft effay, that the coagulability of fluids obeys the fame laws, and depends upon the fame principle as the irritability of the fluids, confequently the blood deprived of the irritable principle, or of

oxy-

oxygene, ought to be liquid, that is, to poffefs, little or no coagulability.

The third experiment is a direct and convincing proof that the florid colour of *arterial blood* is owing to the abforption of oxygene in its paffage through the lungs.

Having fhewn the futility of thofe arguments on which the more generally received theory of refpiration is founded, he proceeds to the ftatement of fome experiments in favour of his new theory.

Experiments upon venous blood.

Firft, Six ounces of black venous blood, taken from the jugular vein of a fheep, were introduced into a veffel filled with oxygene air, and in an inftant the blood affumed a vermilion colour ; the thermometer within the veffel rofe feveral degrees, but funk again immediately. The mercury in

which

which the veffel was placed rofe from fix to eight lines.

When the experiment was finifhed, the blood was encreafed a little in weight; but though I am certain of this encreafe of weight from repeated experiments, I cannot exactly afcertain this encreafe, as the inftruments I made ufe of for this purpofe were not fufficiently accurate for fo delicate an experiment.

The oxygene air which the veffel contained was mixed with carbonic acid air, which lime water abforbed. Some drops of water were formed at the bottom of the veffel.

This experiment feems obvioufly to prove that carbonic acid air and water, are formed during refpiration, or rather that the bafe of hydrogene air is exhaled from the blood.

Secondly, The jugular vein of a fheep was open-

ed

ed and the blood which flowed from it was received in a glafs bottle filled with oxygene air,
and the bottle when half full was clofed. The
blood which it contained immediately affumed a
vermilion colour, became very fluid and coagulated but flowly, into a reddifh and thick mafs,
without any feparation of ferum. The next day
on opening the bottle, in order to examine the air
which it contained, the oxygene air was found
mixed with carbonic acid air. Some drops of water were formed near the mouth of the bottle.
This experiment confirms the firft.

Thirdly, A confiderable quantity of very pure
oxygene air was injected into the jugular vein of
a dog; when the animal raifed the moft terrible
outcries, breathing very quickly, and with the
moft extreme difficulty ; his limbs became gradually ftiff and hard, he fell afleep and died in
lefs than three minutes.

Upon opening the thorax and pericardium,
the

the heart was found more irritable than ordinary, and its alternate contractions and dilatations continued upwards of an hour.

The right auricle of the heart was of a florid red colour and it contained, as also did the right ventricle, a confiderable quantity of blood of a bright vermilion colour, frothy, and not coagulated.

The blood contained in the left ventricle, in the aorta, and the arteries, was of a rofe colour, and mixed with bubbles of air. All the mufcles were more irritable than ordinary ; but after the blood contained in the heart and veins was difcharged, the irritability of the heart and mufcles fenfibly diminifhed.

This experiment appears to me a moft decifive proof that the florid colour which the blood affumes in paffing through the lungs, does not arife from its being deprived of the carbonic hydrogene
air,

air, but that it proceeds from the combination of oxygene air with the blood.

In the experiments we have juft cited, the livid colour of the venous blood in the right auricle and right ventricle of the heart was changed to a more florid red colour. Yet it could not have loft any carbonic hydrogene air ; but only ac-quired oxygene.

This experiment feems alfo to prove that oxy-gene is the principle of irritability ; for by fur-charging the blood with oxygene, the irritabi-lity of the blood was, as we have feen, confider-ably increafed.

Fourthly, A fmall quantity of azotic air, which had been expofed for fome time to the contact of lime water in order to feparate from it any carbo-nic acid air it might contain, was injected into the jugular vein of a dog ; and the animal died in thirty feconds.

2 C

Upon

Upon opening the thorax, the pericardium, and heart, the right auricle and ventricle were filled with black, thick, and coagulated blood. The left ventricle was of its ordinary colour. The heart and nearly all the mufcles loft their irritability almoft entirely ; contracting but feebly upon the application of the ftrongeft ftimuli, fuch as fulphuric æther, and the electric fpark.

5. The venous blood of a fheep was received in a bottle filled with azotic air ; and the blood conftantly coagulated, affuming a colour black as ink, with the feparation of a very confiderable quantity of ferum.

The next day on opening the bottle a faint fmell of ammoniac was perceiveable ; and the air was azotic air, incapable of fupporting flame.

In this experiment the colour of the venous blood was rendered darker and even quite black, by expofure to azotic air.

The

The ammoniac produced was owing to the hydrogene air which had escaped from the venous blood entering into combination with the azote.

Hence, the colour of the blood becoming deeper, after, having lost part of the hydrogene with which it had been charged, would seem to prove that this deepness of colour arose from the presence of carbon in the blood, and not, as has been supposed, from its combination with hydrogene air.

6. A bottle full of carbonic acid air was half filled with the venous blood of a sheep. It coagulated in an instant, assuming a very dark colour; and likewise affording by spontaneous separation a very considerable quantity of a reddish-coloured serum.

7. Having injected a small quantity of carbonic acid gaz into the jugular vein of a dog; the animal fist became sleepy, and died in the course of fifteen minutes.

The

The right auricle and ventricle were found filled with a thick blood, partly coagulated. The blood in the left auricle and ventricle, was of a more deep colour than ordinary ; and the heart and mufcles had loft all their irritability.

This experiment alfo proves that the dark colour of the venous blood is not owing to the combination of hydrogene air.

Perhaps in this experiment, part of the oxygene of the corbonic acid air unites with the hydrogene of the blood, and forms water, and the carbon which was before combined with the oxygene, unites with the blood, and gives it a deeper colour.

8. Blood drawn from the jugular vein of a fheep was received in a bottle full of nitrous air, and when the bottle was half filled it was clofed. The blood immediately took a concrete form, feparating

parating a very confiderable quantity of a blackifh ferum,

The day following, on opening the bottle, a very ftrong fmell of nitrous æther was perceived ;
the nitrous air having been changed in part to nitrous æther by the carbonic-hydrogene air of venous blood.

This experiment would feem to prove beyond
a doubt that venous blood contains carbonic-hydrogene air, and that this air is not very intimately combined therewith, fince it is not fo eafily
feparated from it.

The nitrous æther produced in this experiment arifes from the combination of the carbonic-
hydrogene air. The blood after having loft this
air, does not affume its vermilion colour ; but
on the contrary becomes ftill deeper ; it is not
therefore, to the union of the blood with carbonic-hydrogene, that the peculiar deep colour of

venous

venous blood is owing, fince this colour becomes ftill deeper, on the feparation of hydrogene from the blood.

9. Having injeéted a fmall quantity of nitrous air into the jugular vein of a dog; the animal died in lefs than fix minutes.

The right auricle and ventricle of the heart on examination were found filled with thick, black, and partly coagulated blood. The blood contained in the left ventricle of the heart, was bf a much deeper colour than ordinary ; and the heart had loft its irritability. The lungs were of a greenifh caft, and perfeétly putrefied*. All the canal of the wind-pipe was filled with green foam, which iffued in great quantities from the mouth

* Dr. Beddoes remarks, and we would think, very juftly, that thefe appearances were only a fign of the prefence of nitrous acid, and not of putrefaétion—p. 227.

of

of the animal during the convulfions which pre:
ceded its death.

Experiments upon arterial blood.

10. An incifion was made into the carotid artery of a fheep, and the blood that iffued thence
was received into a bottle full of oxygene air; and
the bottle, when half filled was clofed.

The colour of the blood became in an inftant
of a bright vermilion. The next day the bottle
was opened, and the oxygene gaz which it contained was foud mixed with a very fmall quantity of carbonic acid gaz.

11. The arterial blood from the carotid artery
of a fheep was received into a bottle full of azotic air, and the bottle, when half filled, was clofed.
The blood coagulated at the fame moment and
affumed a very deep colour.

On opening the bottle the next day, the azotic
air

air which it contained was found mixed with a
fmall quantity of oxygene air; rendering it capable of fupporting flame for about two minutes.

This experiment would feem to prove deci-
fively and beyond any poffibility of doubt. Firft,
that arterial blood contains oxygene air, and fe-
condly, that its vermilion colour is produced by
its combination with this air; which colour it
again lofes on being deprived of its oxygene air.

Hence arifes our conviction, of the vaft importance of circulation, and from this theory it may
be no very difficult task to explain almoft every
phenomena of the animal œconomy.

12. Three ounces of vermilion coloured blood,
taken from the carotid artery of a fheep, were
received upon a plate, which was immediately
placed under a veffel filled with carbonic acid
air. The blood did not fuffer any alteration of
colour, but continued the fame for fome hours.

13. Arterial blood, drawn from the carotid artery of a fheep, was received into a bottle filled with carbonic acid air ; but no change of colour took place.

Thefe two laft experiments feem to prove that carbonic acid air, has little or no action upon arterial ; while its influence on the venous blood is very confiderable.

14. Arterial blood, taken from the carotid artery of a fheep was received into a bottle full of nitrous air, and the bottle when half filled was clofed. The blood contained in it coagulated immediately, affuming a green colour upon the furface, and at the fame time feparating a fmall quantity of a greenifh ferum.

The day after, on opening the bottle, the vapours of nitrous acid were obferved by all who were prefent. This experiment feems to prove, in a ftill more decifive manner than any of the

2 D former

former, the prefence of oxygene in the arterial blood ; fince it is from this alone it is capable of changing *nitrous air* into *nitrous acid*.

The green colour, obferved in this, as alfo in the ninth experiment, is owing to a feparation of part of the azote from the nitrous air.

15. Arterial blood, drawn from the carotid artery of a fheep, was received into a bottle full of hydrogene air, which when half filled was clofed. The blood became of a much brighter vermilion, and remained fluid for fome time. It however at laft took a concrete form, and a fmall quantity of ferum was feparated.

On the following day, the hydrogene air contained in the bottle was found mixed with a fmall quantity of oxygene air, which the nitrous air abforbed. This experiment alfo proves the prefence of oxygene air in arterial blood.

16.

16. Arterial blood, was received in a bottle containing equal portions of oxygene and hydrogene air, and the bottle when half filled was clofed. The blood in the bottle became moderately hot, remained fluid, and was of a more bright vermilion colour. It at length coagulated, and a fmall quantity of ferum was feparated.

On examination the day after, the air in the bottle was found mixed with a fmall quantity of carbonic acid air, the prefence of which was afcertained by lime water.

17. A fmall glafs tube was filled with arterial blood of a bright vermilion colour; it was fealed hermetically and expofed to the light. The blood gradually changed colour, and in fix days became as black as venous blood.

18. The fame experiment was repeated, only with this difference, that the tube was expofed to the influence of heat inftead of light, but with-

out

out any other difference in the refult, than that of the fame effect being produced in a much fhorter time.

The 17th and 18th experiments made by Dr. Prieftly, and afterwards repeated, feem to demonftrate, that it is not from the contact with hydrogene air that the venous is of a more deep colour than that of the arterial blood.

From thefe experiments he concludes—

1. That the change of colour the blood undergoes during circulation is not owing to its combinations with hydrogene air.

2. That the deep colour of the venous blood is owing to the carbon it contains.

3. That the vermilion colour of the arterial blood proceeds from the oxygene with which the blood is combined, during its paffage through the lungs.

4.

4. That refpiration is a procefs exactly analogous to the combuftion and oxidation of metals;
that thefe phenomena are the fame, and to be explained in the fame manner.

5. That during circulation, the blood lofes its
oxygene, and charges itfelf with carbonic-hydrogene air, by means of a double affinity.

6. That during the diftribution of the oxygene
through the fyftem, the heat which was united
with this oxygene efcapes; hence the phenomena
of animal heat, &c.

7. That the great capacity of the arterial blood
for heat is owing to the oxygene with which it is
united in the lungs.

Having pretty clearly demonftrated that the
blood is oxygenated in its paffage through the
lungs; that in the courfe of circulation it becomes
deprived of the oxygene which it had abforbed
from

from the atmofphere ; and that it returns to the lungs furcharged with carbonic-hydrogene air, it now remains to prove that this oxygene gives rife to irritability, and the life of organized bodies.—And the following are proofs on which he founds this theory.

The irritability of all organized bodies is in a direct ratio of the quantity of oxygene they contain.

1. Whatever increafes the quantity of oxygene in organized bodies, at the fame time increafes their irritability.

In the third experiment above cited we have feen a direct proof of this, and other phenomena feem obvioufly to favour his opinion. Animals made to breath oxygene air have their irritability very confiderably encreafed. Blanched plants, whofe irritability has been accumulated in confequence of the abftraction of light, contain (according

cording to the experiments of Mr. Fourcroy) a very confiderable quantity of oxygene.

Dr. Girtanner obferved, that in the courfe of his experiments, plants made to grow in oxygene air, became white, although expofed to the influence of the light.

But what feem more forcible proofs of irritability being always in proportion to the quantity of oxygene, are the phenomena attendant on the action of mercury and mercurial falts upon animals.

This being one of the moft ftriking proofs of his theory it may not be unworthy of our taking notice of it at fome length.

It is a fact, he obferves well known by phyficians, that mercury, in its metallic ftate, has no effect upon the human body ; many people have been known to take a daily portion of quickfil-

ver,

ver, to the amount of two or three ounces, for years, from the idea of its guarding them againſt epidemic diſeaſes, but who could never perceive any ſenſible effect whatever from ſo ſingular a cuſtom.

The experiments of Dr. Saunders alſo prove, that the effects of mercurial ointment are owing only to the ſmall quantity of mercury that has been oxidated in the courſe of a long trituration. Hence we would conclude, that it is neceſſary mercury ſhould be oxidated, in order to have any effect upon the human body.

On the other hand, it is well known that in perſons who have rubbed themſelves with mercurial ointment, or who have taken the oxid of mercury internally, the mercury, after having produced its uſual effects upon the ſyſtem, has paſſed through the pores of the skin in a metallic form, and has amalgamated itſelf with watches, gold in the pocket, &c.

The

The oxid of mercury, in paffing through the human body becomes deprived of its oxygene, and to this oxygene alone, which remains combined with the fyftem, are owing the effects produced by oxidated mercury.

Thefe effects he calls the mercurial difeafe, the fymptoms of which are nearly the fame as thofe of fcurvy ; the mouth, gums, and whole fyftem becoming affected in a manner extremely analogous.

But the fcurvy he obferves, is a difeafe produced by the accumulation of the irritable principle*. The accumulation therefore of the oxygene producing the fame effects, the ftriking analogy between the irritable principle and oxy-

* The Doctor's opinion in this inftance is certainly very erroneous, fince it is, I believe, from the *want* of oxygene (which he confiders the principle of irritability) that this difeafe takes its rife.

2 E

gene

gene appears to be proved ; and from hence he concludes, that oxygene is the principle of irritability†.

2. Every thing that diminifhes the quantity of oxygene in organized bodies, at the fame time, diminifhes their irritability.

This was clearly demonftrated in the 9th experiment where the heart and mufcles loft their irritability, on being deprived of their oxygene by nitrous acid. But to put this beyond a doubt he inftituted the following experiment.

Exp. 19. The heart of an animal juft killed was cut into pieces, and put into a glafs retort, to which was affixed a pneumatic apparatus. A very fmall degree of heat was applied to it, by means of a lamp placed under the retort. When

---

† M. Bertholet, in the Paris Memoirs, for the year 1788, has attributed the caufticity of metallic oxids to the hydrogene they contain.

the

the pieces were heated, bubbles of air were perceived in the pneumatic apparatus. They remained expofed to the fame degree of heat for nearly two hours, till the furface was juft burnt.

Upon examining the air which had paffed into the
apparatus, it was found that the firft portion of air
was the atmofpheric air of the retort, mixed with a
very fmall quantity of vital or oxygene air, the prefence of which was afcertained by nitrous air; the
fecond was vital air mixed with carbonic acid air.

He repeated this experiment upon various o-
ther parts of animals recently killed, always ob-
taining a greater or lefs quantity of oxygene air.

The fame quantity of this air, he obferves, may
be obtained, for many fucceffive times, by expofure of the animal fubftance, alternately to atmofpheric air and a heat equal to 60° or 70° of
Reaumur's fcale. He remarks that thefe experiments are very difficult, and require fome time

to

to afcertain the degree of heat neceffary to difen-
gage the oxygene air, for if the degree of heat
applied be too great, inftead of oxygene air, carbonic acid air will be forced over.

From the foregoing obfervations it may be collected, that oxygene combines with the venous
blood in the lungs ; that it is diftributed to every
part of the fyftem in the courfe of circulation,
and that to this principle irritability is owing ;
it remains only to examine what becomes of the
vaft quantity of oxygene, which all parts of the
fyftem are continually receiving from the blood.

In his firft memoir he has obferved that there
are three different ftates of the organized fibre.

1. The ftate of health or tone of the fibre.

2. The ftate of accumulation, in which the
fibre has become furcharged with the irritable
principle.

3. The

3. The state of exhaustion, in which the fibre fails through want of the irritable principle.

Every substance capable of coming in contact with the irritable fibre, may likewise be arranged under three classes, of which,

The *first* comprehends those substances which have the same degree of affinity to the irritable principle, or oxygene, as the organized fibre itself. These substances produce no effect upon the fibre.

The *second* contains those which have a less degree of affinity to the oxygene, than what the fibre has. These substances coming in contact with the fibre, will surcharge it with oxygene and produce the state of accumulation, and which substances may be called *negative* stimuli.

The *third* class contains those substances which have a greater degree of affinity to the oxygene, than

than even the fibre itfelf has. Thefe coming in contact with the fibre, will of courfe deprive it of its oxygene, and produce the ftate of exhauftion. And thefe fubftances he calls *pofitive* ftimuli.

It is a fact known at this time, that the affinity of different fubftances varies very confiderably according to the degree of temperature, and the fame variations take place in the organized fibre. It may not therefore be irrelavant to obferve that in fpeaking generally of the affinities of the irrita-ble fibre, he means always in the ordinary tempe-rature of the blood in warm animals.

The firft clafs comprehends, as we have ob-ferved, fubftances having the fame degree of affi-nity to the oxygene as the irritable fibre. All organized, or living fubftances are to be ranked under this clafs*. Thefe fubftances produce no

---

* The words *organized* and *living*, he confiders as fynoni-mous, regarding as living, every body, each part of any body, in a word, all organized fubftances, as long as they

effect

effect upon the irritable fibre, while their degree of temperature is the fame as that of the fibre with which they come in contact.

In the third clafs are arranged the *pofitive* ſti-muli, or thofe fubftances which have a greater affinity to the oxygene, than what the fibre has. Thefe fubftances coming in contact with the fibre combine with the oxygene it contains, deprive it of its irritabily, and leave it in a ftate of exhauſ-tion; of thefe fubftances there are a very confidera-ble number, and of which the moft general ones are alcohol, fulphuric æther, opium, and other narcotics, oil of lauto-cerafus, and oils in general, greafe, fugar, &c.

contain the principle of irritability, or of life, and as long as the affinities are the fame as thofe of living fubftances. The wood, for inftance, of which our chairs and tables are made, is an organized or living fubftance, and to fpeak pro-perly, it cannot be faid that the wood is dead until it is actually decayed, and fo of the reft.

All

All thefe fubftances are combuftible, having a great affinity to oxygene, and from this property it is that they deprive the organized fibre of its irritability, by combining with the oxygene it contains.

The fecond clafs, we have faid, comprehends the negative ftimuli, or fubftances which have a lefs affinity to the oxygene, than what the fibre has. And under this clafs muft be ranked fome of the moft terrible poifons with which we are acquainted.

The oxygene which combines with the organized fibre, when it comes in contact with thefe poifons, renders it fo extremely irritable, that the weakeft ftimulus is capable of producing death; by a law of irritability which has already been explained.

It is on this account that *oxygenated marine acid* is fo fatal a poifon to all organized bodies. It
deftroys

deftroys them by furcharging them with irritability, and becomes *marine acid* by this operation.

Arfenic, in its metallic ftate, has no effect upon animals; but the white oxid of this metal is
one of the moft dreadful poifons, for it hyper-
oxygenates the organized fibre with which it
comes in contact, re-affuming its metallic form.

Similar effects are produced by the oxygenated
metallic falts, as oxygenated muriatic fublimate of
mercury, &c.

The oxids of filver and mercury produce greater or lefs effect upon the organized fibre, in proportion as they contain more or lefs oxygene.
The black oxid of mercury, otherwife called
æthiops, produces but very trifling effects; but
the moft terrible effects are produced from the red
oxid of this metal, which deftroys organized bodies in a very fhort time.

2 F   The

The fame explanation, applies equally to the action of fulphate of tin, and of lead ; as alfo to that of the acetate of lead and of brafs upon the organized fibre.

Dr. Girtanner feems fully convinced that the organized fibre, both of animals and vegetables, decompofes the water with which it comes in contact, the greateft portion of the water we drink being firft decompofed, and afterwards re-compofed.

It is indeed one of the means by which nature furnifhes organized bodies with the oxygene neceffary to the prefervation of their irritability and life. And on this difcovery, many phenomena hitherto inexplicable may readily be explained ; perhaps too that æra is not far diftant, when from thefe important difcoveries we may be enabled to deduce an explication of the moft hidden myfteries of animal phyfiology.

The

The fame author fuppofes that the hydrogene air which remains, after the oxygene of the water is united to the irritable fibre, may ferve to fupply the lofs of nervous fluid, or rather that this hydrogene air, is itfelf the nervous fluid, or perhaps carbonic hydrogene air.

We have already remarked that the fenfation of hunger in animals, was the confequence of irritability accumulated in the fyftem; and that in order for any fubftance to be nutritious, it muft be a pofitive ftimulus; or one that has a very confiderable tendency to combine with the oxygene, fince it is only by its union with this principle, with which the fyftem is furcharged, that it can be enabled to reftore the tone of the fibre, and allay the painful fenfation of hunger..

Every phenomenon feems to fupport this theory; different fubftances nourifhing only in pro. proportion to their affinity with oxygene living animal fubftances, as oyfters, &c. afford but very

little

little nourifhment, becaufe they cannot combine with the oxygene, being already faturated with that principle; hence the common obfervation, that oyfters encreafe the appetite.

Animal jellies, fruits, and vegetable fubftances, in general afford very little nourifhment. Animal food recently killed, does not afford equal nutrition with that which has been kept fome time; nor is raw meat fo nourifhing as that which has been cooked. Hence all the art of cookery confifts in depriving the food of its oxygene, by the application of different ftimulating fubftances, and efpecially the ftimulus of heat.

Roafting, is perhaps the moft fimple mode of cooking the food; by expofure to heat, it parts with its oxygene, as in the 19th experiment.

Oils, fat, fugar, alcohol, and other fubftances which have a great affinity to oxygene, are very nourifhing. And in the Eaft-Indies, millions of

men

men are fupported, folely by fmall quantities of opium, when the rice harveft fails them, as is very frequently the cafe in thofe wretched coun-tries groaning under the defpotifm of a company of * * merchants.

Thirft is a ftate of the fyftem very oppofite to that of hunger; it is a fenfation which induces a ftate of exhauftion, or in other words, a deficien-cy of oxygene.

Every thing that is capable of reftoring to the fibre its loft oxygene, puts an end to this difagree-able fenfation. Water produces this effect by its decompofition which takes place when it comes in contact with the fibre.

The fame effect will be produced by the vege-table acids, which are always decompofed in the ftomach of animals.

It

It is only in proportion to the quantity of oxygene which enters into the compofition of the acid, and to which they have but little affinity, that they refrefh and allay the fenfation of thirft.

Thus vegetable acids are the moft powerful remedies againft the effects of narcotic poifons; for by their decompofition they reftore to the fibre an equal quantity of oxygene with that of which it had been deprived by the poifon.

Vinegar taken in large dofes, caufes the ftate of exhauftion produced by a ftrong dofe of opium, and prevents death, which might otherwife enfue.

It is a well known fact, that drunken perfons, become lefs inebriated, by drinking a glafs of vinegar, reftoring the tone of the fyftem which had been loft by the effect of the alcohol contained in the wine. Water, only in much more confiderable quantities, will produce the fame effect.

Per-

Perhaps many other phenomena are to be explained upon the fame principles.

The phenomena difplayed by the rotifer are indeed truly aftonifhing; that fingular infect, though
entirely dried up, may be revived by moiftening
it with a drop of water; this phenomena which
hath hitherto appeared inexplicable, would feem
eafily to be accounted for on thefe principles.

The drop of water becomes decompofed, and
the oxygene which it contained combining with
the rotifer, reftores its irritability, its life, and organic motion, of which it have been deprived by
the ftimulus of heat, to which it had been expofed in becoming dry.

Among the known poffitive ftimuli thofe which
are capable of producing the greateft effects are
the ftimuli of putrid fevers, or of the plague, and
that of the mephitis, which is exhaled during the
putrefaction of animal fubftances, in places where
atmof.

atmofpheric air cannot enter, as in tombs and burial places, &c.

This mephitic gaz has fo great an affinity with oxygene, that as foon as it comes in contact with the fibre, it deprives it of its oxygene, and produces death, frequently in an inftant. The moft efficacious mode of preventing the fatal effects of this gaz is by the detonation of nitre upon burning charcoal.

During the decompofition of the nitre a confiderable quantity of oxygene air efcapes, and fupplies the oxygene which combines with the mephitic air. This theory would feem fully proved, from the workmen who have been fuffocated by the mephitic air exhaling from tombs, having (to ufe their own expreffions) recovered their fenfes and been refrefhed, as foon as they have been made to refpire oxygene air.

Dr. Girtanner found that many ftimulating

fubsubstances, but more especially alcohol, opium, the solution of white oxid of arsenic, vinegar, water, heat, and the oxid of mercury, produced similar effects upon plants as they had done upon animals ; that the most irritable plants, such as the mimosa and hedisarum, may be entirely destroyed by positive stimuli, as for instance, by opium, alcohol or heat, and that it is possible to give very sensible irritability to plants, which did not *a priori* appear to possess it, by applying, for some time, negative stimuli, such as vinegar, or white oxid of arsenic.

He observes, that he has found oils, and alcohol, when used in small quantities, are specific remedies for the diseases of plants, produced by accumulation of the irritable principle; diseases which are marked by the yellow colour of the leaves.

It may very naturally be expected that numerous hints of no inconsiderable utility to medicine

2 G

and

and agriculture, may be collected from thefe difcoveries, by fhewing us the true nature of animals
and plants, their feveral difeafes, and the means of
remedying them.

This theory of Dr. Girtanner's, like that of every
other which preceded it, is not without its pal-
pable defects.

We cannot fuppofe that any fubftance which
directly, and without any appearance of previous
excitement, in whatever quantity they are adminiftered, fuch as lead diminifhes the action of life,
is a lefs powerful ftimulus ; for in what manner,
on this principle, can they diminifh the effect of
the ordinary ftimuli, which are applied at the fame
time ?

It is equally well obferved by Dr. Beddoes that
univerfal experience muft immediately reject his
idea of the depreffing paffions being only the abftraction of the ftimuli of the exciting paffions.

We

We muft, fays Dr. Beddoes, where obfervation indicates it, admic a power in fome drugs, in fome of the paffions, and in fome external circumftances, either of preventing the fyftem from giving out its excitability, or from accumulating it, (which ftate is very often feen, where a continuance of fleep fufficient as to its duration does not refrefh, or according to Dr. Cullen's expreffion, *render the fyftem more liable to be affected by ftimuli of all kinds*), or on the contrary, of accumulating it too rapidly. We are even enabled by the foregoing hypothefis to conceive a modus operandi in all thefe cafes.

Thefe principles, fays he, with which the late wonderful difcoveries of Galvani, Valli, and Volta, feem perfectly well difpofed to coalefce, promife all thofe advantages which would refult from a perfect knowledge of the mechanifm of the animal functions.

Was not Mayow, fays he, infinitely nearer the
truth,

truth, than any author of a later hypothefis when he attributed mufcular motion to the *effervefcence of his nitro-atmofpherical particles* ? Does not mufcular contraction or intumefcence really depend upon the combination of oxygene with hydrogene and azote (feparately and combined, in various proportions), in confequence of a fort of explofion produced by the nervous electricity ?

According to this hypothefis, animal motion, at leaft that of animals analogous to man, would be produced by a very beautiful pneumatic machinery ; and our nervous and mufcular fyftems may be confidered as a fort of fteam engine.

Although this hypothefis, may not at this moment be capable of ftrict and fufficient proof, yet it is not only extremely probable but alfo would feem to be fupported by every obfervation and experiment yet made upon the fubject.

It accounts for the continual neceffity of our

in-

inhaling oxygene and enables us to trace the changes which this fubftance undergoes, from the
moment of its being received to that of its expulfion.

By the blood it is imparted to the mufcular
fibres; and during their contraction combines
with the elements above mentioned, into water
and various falts, among which the marine and
phofphoric acids deferve particular notice; and
of which, as exifting in the blood, &c. we have
already had occafion to fpeak, in a former part
of this effay.

From thofe few obfervations cited in the preceding pages, we may be very eafily convinced of
the immediate neceffity of oxygene to mufcular
motion; and that where this principle is not
fupplied in fufficient quantity, the power of motion will be proportionately languid.

Dr. Beddoes remarks that *meat* becomes tender

by

by the fecondary combination of oxygene, in whatever manner this fecondary combination be effected ; whether by keeping it till the putrefactive
procefs takes place more or lefs ; by cookery ;
by obliging the animal to undergo violent exercife before death, as in hare-hunting, bull-baiting
and in an expedient of gluttony, rather more
barbarous than either of the preceding, that of
flogging poultry to death.

The flefh of animals fo deftroyed ought alfo
to be more fucculent, as well as more tender.

Many experienced fportfmen have obferved that
an hunted hare will continue to emit fteam, for
a much more confiderable time, after being
brought to table, than an hare killed by any other
means, and myfelf as well as others have *frequently*
heard the fame remark in regard to hunted
venifon.

Thefe phenomena correfpond perfectly with the
fup-

fuppofition of liquids partly volatile, being generated during mufcular action.

In the Weft Indies, it is a very frequent cuftom to kill their poultry with vegetable poifon,
in order to render them tender without keeping,
and various ftimuli, which are only lefs violent -
poifons, are occafionally ufed for the fame purpofe
in this country. It is not afcertained with certainty, whether they produce their effects immediately or by firft exciting the nervous electricity.

But whatever be the direct mode of action of
thefe ftimuli and poifons, that of contagious miaf-
mata would feem to be exactly the fame.

Dr. Beddoes relates a cafe in which he could
not doubt that complete intoxication was produced by the contagion of typhus, to which
the perfon had been much expofed.

" One morning, immediately upon rifing, and

I

I know that he had been perfectly fober the night before, I was aftonifhed to obferve that flighty vivacity and difpofition to wild disjointed talk, together with the other figns which infallibly denote a certain degree of intoxication, efpecially when you are well acquainted before hand with the manners of the party. In the courfe of the day, during which I faw him frequently, he became heavy, had febrile fhiverings, and complained of the head ache.

" The next day he became more feverifh, but was not confined till the fifth day, though the headache, and other fymptoms never quitted him. He paffed through all the ftages of typhus, but never feemed to be in imminent danger."

To this the Doctor adds what we would deem a very important obfervation; " That, in moft inftances, the period of the excitement of the brain is not perceived ; we however, frequently fee the action of the vofcular fyftem increafed at

gene-the onſet of typhus. This increaſe of action ſometimes miſleads practitioners into the fatal meaſure of blood-letting.

The ſame author ſuppoſes, and perhaps with every degree of truth which analogy might afford, that the more highly ſaline ſtate of the wine in febrile diſeaſes, and after exerciſe, depends on the chemical combinations above mentioned.

The ſimilarity of ſymptoms in typhus and ſcurvy has frequently been noticed ; and the ſimilar ſymptoms of theſe diſeaſes ſeem evidently to depend upon the ſame cauſe ; the contagion of typhus depriving the ſyſtem of oxygene, by producing the combination of a great part of that which it already contains. Hence, as Dr. Beddoes very aptly obſerves, it is probable that the true indication of cure in typhus is to reſtore the oxygene; and it is highly probable that upon this principle, a certain and ſpeedy cure may ere long be contrived.

2 H   The

The prefent ftate of modern practice which au-
thorizes the, perhaps too liberal ufe of ftimulants,
though, certainly upon the whole more beneficial
than the contrary, is yet by no means fuch as we
ought tacitly to acquiefce in. It does not enfure
fo much fuccefs as might be expected from a method founded on juft and invariable principles;
and perhaps the different methods in ufe anfwer
pretty much alike, the difeafe being but little
in the power of the phyfician.

Oxygene may be more beneficial at one ftage
of typhus than at another.

Thofe cafes in which typhus fupervenes after
expofure to fevere cold, at a time when it is im-
poffible, by the ftricteft fcrutiny to difcover any
previous veftiges of contagion in the neighbour-
hood, render it highly probable that this difeafe
may be produced by ordinary ftimuli when applied to excitability much accumulated.

The

The fymptoms of the influenza, which are very
difficultly to be diftinguifhed from thofe of catarrh,
as well as the effect produced by the Steward's
vifit to the natives of St. Kilda, (if this refpec-
tably attefted, though furprizing narrative be
true) afford another inftance where difeafes, extremely fimilar at leaft, are produced by ordinary
ftimuli, and by the extraordinary ftimulus of
contagion.

If the marfh-miafma be not an imaginary being,
there is reafon to prefume the fame thing of in-
termittents, which very often appear where marfh-
miafma cannot well be fuppofed to exift.

It is very probable that the feverifh fymptoms,
or indirect debility, which very generally, or
rather perhaps in every inftance, fucceed to intoxication, may be relieved, or perhaps entirely removed, by the perfons being made to refpire oxygene air.

This,

This, Dr Beddoes fuppofes, would not only make up the want of this principle, but might alfo reftore the nervous electricity ; a circumftance to which it will no doubt be always neceffary to attend in diforders of excitement, or fuch as are produced by excitement.

I have myfelf found an almoft immediate alleviation of thofe fymptoms which attend a flight degree of inebriety, by the detonation of nitre upon burning charcoal; but as we are now engaged in fome experiments which have not been profecuted a fufficient length to authorize any certain conclufions therefrom, we fhall defer entering into the fubject more particularly in this place, but fhall take an opportunity of giving their refult to the world in a future publication.

From the experiments of Meffrs. Sauffure and Volta, on the electrical phenomena attending condenfation, Dr. B. thinks it may reafonably be

con-

conjectured that animal electricity is renewed by respiration. The want, he adds, of some certain method to effect this may, perhaps, give rise to some doubt in the mind of the reader, respecting the certain efficacy of an hyper-oxygenated atmosphere in typhus ; but the few trials that have hitherto been made upon the respiration of oxygene air, seem to him more than adequate to counterballance this doubt.

From what has been advanced in the foregoing pages, we may readily infer that the gaseous substance, called by Dr. Priestly *vital air*, and by modern chemists *oxygene gaz*, is perhaps the most essentially necessary agent in the numerous operations of the animal œconomy.

We find it existing in combination with a variety of substances; and from which it is very readily procured by their decomposition.

Some

Some metallic oxids yield this gaz in a very pure ſtate, by ſimple diſtillation, and receiving it in the hydro-pneumatic apparatus. Thus from one ounce of the red precipitate, or *oxidum bydrargyri rubrum acido nitrico confeĉtum,* near a pint of gaz may be obtained.

It is this gaz which conſtitutes the baſe of all acids, and from ſome of which it is very eaſily ſeparable.

Thus from one pound of nitre may be obtained twelve hundred cubic inches, or thereabout, of oxygenous gaz, which is ſet at liberty by the decompoſition of the nitric acid.

Plants and vegetables likewiſe, when in a ſtate of health and expoſed to the light of the ſun, emit vital air*.

* This curious faĉt was firſt noticed by Prieſtly, Ingenhouſz, and Senebier.

This

This air may be readily procured from plants, by enclofing them beneath a glafs veffel full of water, inverted over a tub filled with the fame fluid. As foon as the plant is acted upon by the fun, fmall air bubbles will be obferved forming on its leaves which foon detach themfelves, and rif- ing to the fuperior part of the veffel, difplace the liquid.

Hence it would appear that the animal and ve- getable kingdoms are not fupported by one and the fame principle ; for while plants abforb azotic gaz or atmofpheric mephitis, and emit vital or oxygenous air, man, on the contrary, exhales a confiderable quantity of mephitis, and owes the continuance of his exiftence to the abforptionj of oxygene or vital air, and thus by a kind of reci- procity of fervices the two kingdoms would feem to labour for each other*.

---

* Vide Chaptal's Elements of Chemiftry, tranflated by Nicholfon.

Oxy-

Oxygene gaz exhibits certain properties according to its degree of purity, and the fubftances
which afford it. That which is obtained from
mercurial oxids, M. Chaptal fuppofes, always
holds in folution a fmall quantity of mercury;
and he obferves that in two cafes he has been wit-
nefs to its having produced a fpeedy falivation,
when ufed for diforders of the lungs.

We have before remarked that oxygene gaz
was neceffary to the procefs of combuftion; nor
indeed can any combuftion take place without
the prefence of this gaz.

In the procefs of moft combuftions oxygene
gaz becomes concrete, fetting at liberty the caloric principle to which its aëriform ftate was owing. Thus being forced from its former combination it produces heat, endeavouring to combine
with the neareft fubftances.

It

It is this gaz alone which is proper for refpiration, and from this peculiar and moſt eminent
property its firſt diſcoverer* gives it the name of
vital air.

In a former part of this work we have had occaſion to ſpeak ſomewhat fully on the phenomena
of reſpiration ; yet we truſt the majority of our
readers will not deem it unneceſſary or unintereſt-
ing that we ſhould here make ſome curſory obſervations on that important function.

The ancients ſeem to have been fully ſenſible
of its connection with the welfare of animal life.
They admitted in the air a principle neceſſary to
the ſupport of life, which they termed *pabulum
vitæ* and Hippocrates himſelf expreſsly ſays, *ſpiritus
etiam alimentum eſt.*

---

* It was diſcovered by the celebrated Dr. Prieſtly on the
memorable 1ſt of Auguſt, 1774.

Vari-

Various have been the fyftems which have fucceeded to that idea, all equally void of reafon or
foundation.—Sometimes the air was fuppofed to
be a ftimulus in the lungs, neceffary to keep up
the circulation by its continual action*.

By others the lungs have been confidered as a
fort of bellows defigned to cool the body, previoufly heated by a thoufand imaginary caufes ; and
upon its being proved that the volume of air was
diminifhed in the lungs, every difficulty was
thought to be cleared up, by faying that the air
was deprived of its elafticity.

Modern experiments and obfervations have
however thrown very confiderable light on this
moft important function of the human body.

I believe it is univerfally admitted that no animal can live without the affiftance of air, but the
difcovery is but of modern date, which has given

* Vide Haller.

rife

rife to our prefent knowledge concerning 'that principle in the atmofphere, more effentially ferviceable for the purpofes of refpiration, and to which has been given the appellation of vital air or oxygenous gaz. But the fame degree of purity in the air is not required in all animals. Birds, men, and the greater number of quadrupeds, require a very pure air ; but fuch animals 'as live in the earth or hide themfelves in a dormant, or ftupefactive ftate during winter, do not require fo pure an air as neceffary to their exiftence.

Thefe are not the only circumftances in which the ftate of refpiration in the varieties of animals differ. The very *mode* of refpiring air varies in different fubjects.

Moft animals are fupplied with an organ, for the purpofe of receiving the fluid in which the animal lives, and expelling from the fyftem fuch matters as are become ufelefs, or deleterious thereto: and according to Mr. Brouffonnet is more

or

or. lefs perfect, and defended from external injury in proportion to its importance and influence upon the life of the individual.

M. Chaptal obferves that although amphibious animals refpire by means of lungs, yet can they fufpend the action of thefe organs even while they are in the air ; particularly frogs, which he fays, can ftop their refpiration at pleafure.

Fifhes refpire in a very different manner from moft animals. They are under the neceffity of coming from time to time to the furface of the water, for the purpofe of inhaling air, with which having filled their veficle they retire to digeft it, ad libitum.

The laft mentioned author, having paid very minute attention, and for a confiderable time, to the phenomena of refpiration in fifhes, concludes that they are fenfible to the action of all the gazes, in like manner as all other animals. It has been

ob-

obferved by M. de Fourcroy, that the air contained in the veficle of a carp is nitrogene gaz*.

The refpiratory organs of infects are ftill more
imperfect than thofe of man ; exhibiting many
very ftriking marks of analogy with vegetables.

The formation of their organs are particularly
fimilar, being difpofed alike throughout the whole
body of the animal and vegetable, nor do infects
require the air to be particularly pure; and
plants, we have obferved, are nourifhed with atmofpheric mephitis ; but both plants and infects
tranfpire oxygenous gaz, or vital air†.

* The *Phlogifticated air* of Dr. Prieftly.

† The Abbé Fontana difcovered feveral infects in ftagnated
waters, which, when expofed to the fun, afforded vital air:
and the green matter which is formed in ftagnant water,
and placed by Dr. Prieftly among the confervæ, in confor-
mity with the opinion of Bewley—which was fuppofed by
Mr. Senebier to be the *conferva cefpitofa filis rectis undique di-*

Thefe

Thefe are not the only circumftances in which fimilarity is found to exift; for by chemical ana-lyfis principles may be obtained from infects, fi-milar to thofe of plants, as refins, volatile oils, &c.

Animals, on the contrary, are capable of ref-piring only from the affiftance of oxygene air, on the proportion of which alone depends their free-dom of refpiration. The experiments of Count Morozzo fully confirm this*, and from them it may be concluded—

vergentibus Halleri, and which has appeared to Dr. Ingen-houfz to be nothing elfe than a mafs of animalcula—affords a prodigious quantity of this air when expofed to the fun.

* He placed fucceffively feveral full grown fparrows un-der a glafs bell, inverted over water. At firft it was filled with atmofpheric air, and afterwards with oxygene gaz, or vital air. He obferved firft in atmofpheric air, that—

	Hours.	Minutes.
The firft fparrow lived —	3	o
The Second — — —	o	3
The third — — —	o	1

I.

1. That animals live longer in vital, than atmofpheric air. 2. That an animal can live in air in which another has died. 3. That independent of the nature of the air, refpect muft be had to the conftitution of the animal*. 4. That there is

During the life of the firft the water rofe in the veffel eight lines ; and during the life of the fecond, four ; but no abforption was produced by the third. He then filled the veffel with vital air, in which—

		Hours.	Minutes.
The firft fparrow lived	—	5	23
The fecond	— —	2	10
The third	— —	1	30
The fourth	— —	1	10
The fifth	— —	0	30
The Sixth	— —	0	47
The feventh	— —	0	27
The eighth	— —	0	30
The ninth	— —	0	22
The tenth	— —	0	21

* This appears from the *fixth* fparrow having furvived 47 minutes, and the *fifth* only thirty.

an

an abforption of air, or a production of a new kind of air, which as it rifes is ablorbed by the water†.

If the expired air which iffues from the lungs be made to pafs through lime water, it renders it turbid ; if through tincture of turnfole, it reddens it ; and if pure alkali be fubftituted in place of the latter, it becomes effervefcent.

The carbonic acid is abforbed in the foregoing procefs, leaving nitrogene gaz and vital air. The prefence of which laft is afcertained by nitrous air.

Frugivorous or graminivorous animals have been obferved to vitiate the air lefs than carnivorous animals.

Borelli formerly obferved that a portion of the air is abforbed in refpiration ; which the ex-

† Vide Chaptal's Chemiftry.

periments

periments of Dr. Jurin* confirmed, but the celebrated Dr. Hales‡ endeavoured to afcertain this
abforption more accurately ; yet as he paffed the
expired air through water, his procefs could not
be fufficiently depended on.

M. De la Metherie has proved, by more accurate experiments, that three hundred and fixty cubic inches of vital air are abforbed in the courfe of
one hour ; perhaps however the confumption is
not near fo great—However that may be, it affords fufficient proof of the facility with which air
is vitiated by refpiration if it is not renewed,
and confirms what we have before had occafion
to fay with regard to the air of theatres, &c. being
in general fo extremely unwholefome.—And further, by air which has been kept in contact with
blood, being incapable of fupporting flame, and
by its precipitating lime-water.

* Deffert. 4. Lib. 4.

‡ Veget. Staties, Vol. 2nd—See alfo *Borelli* de Motu Animal, Lib. 11—*Sauvage* de Refpiratione difficili.—*Bernoulli*
Differt. de Refpiratione.

The

The influence of vital or oxygene air upon the blood is confirmed by the teftimony of fo many and refpectable authors as fcarcely to leave room for the fmalleft degree of doubt. M. Thouvenal has proved that by exhaufting the air from its contact with the blood, it will be again deprived of its colour; which Mr. Beccaria alfo confirmed by expofing blood in a vacuum, where the blood remained black, but upon admitting the air it af-fumed a moft beautiful vermilion colour.

M. Cigna having covered blood with oil, found that it preferved its black colour.

Dr. Prieftly alfo found that the intenfity of the colour of blood was in proportion to the quantity of vital air*. From all thefe facts, it appears to be inconteftibly demonftrated that the bright co-

* Dr. Prieftly having filled a bladder with blood, and ex-pofed it to the influence of vital air, found that portion of blood which touched the furface of the bladder, affumed a red colour, while the internal part remained black.

lour

lour of the blood is folely owing to its combination with oxygene air.

We have already took occafion to remark, that
animal heat was derived to the fyftem from this
combination, but we might go ftill further, and
add from the obfervations of the Count De Buffon
and M. Brouffonnet, that the heat in every individual animal, is proportionate to the fize of the
lungs.

Hence M. Chaptal confiders refpiration as an
operation by means of which vital air paffes continually from the gafeous to the concrete ftate,
fetting at liberty the heat, which held it in the
ftate of gaz. But the heat produced at each
infpiration, muft uniformly be in proportion to
the volume of the lungs, to the action of this organ, to the purity of the air, and to the rapidity
and frequency of the infpirations, &c. Hence the
lungs of afthmatic perfons are incapable of di-
gefting the air in a proper manner, infomuch that

it

it has been obferved they emit the air without vitiating it, producing coldnefs of the complexion, &c. and a languid ftate of the refpiratory organs; vital air is therefore peculiarly grateful to them. From hence we may readily conceive why animal heat is in proportion to the volume of the lungs; and why fuch animals as have only one auricle and ventricle, have cold blood, &c.

By the combination of oxygene air with the blood, we have obferved, carbonic acid is formed, which fo long as it remains in the fyftem may be confidered as antifeptic; and according to the experiments and obfervations of the Count De Milly, and Mr. Fouquet, it is afterwards paffed off through the pores of the skin.

Thus vital air or oxygenous gaz, from its very intimate connection with many of the vital functions, may open a vaft field for improvement in the practice of medicine. It has been tried very frequently, efpecially in phthifical diforders, and

al-

although it does not appear to be adapted to
such cases, yet it has been found to infpire cheer-
fulnefs, and render the patient happy ; at leaft,
in defperate cafes, it is moft certainly a precious
remedy, " which can fpread flowers on the bor-
ders of the tomb, and perpare us in the gentleft
manner for the laft dreadful effort of nature."

It were much to be wifhed that the nature of
the various alterations which take place in the
blood were better afcertained by accurate analyfis
rather, than that phyficians fhould be left to judge
of thefe varieties merely by external appearances;
efpecially in the different difeafes, which produce
the more peculiar and confiderable alterations in
this fluid ; as in ftrong inflammations, chlorofis,
fcorbutic diforders, &c.

From the preceding analyfis of the blood arifes
that knowledge which we at prefent have of that
fluid ; and hence we may find it to be compofed
of a variety of particles, differing in bulk, denfity

fity, figure and tenacity ; fome aqueous, others inflammable ; and moft of them much inclined to putrefaction, and of an alkaline nature.

The exact quantity of blood contained in a living animal, cannot be exactly computed, but it is very generally believed, that the mafs of humours very much exceeds that of the folids ; although it is to be obferved, that fome of them as the gluten and fat of particular parts, do not flow in the circulation : but if from thofe profufe hæmorrhagies which have been fuftained without affecting the deftruction of animal life, and from experiments made on animals by drawing out all, or as much as poffible of their blood, the circulating humours will be found to amount, to at leaft fifty pounds ; of which mafs twenty eight pounds will be true red blood circulating through the arterial and venous fyftems, the former containing four parts, and the latter nine.

But the blood does not always contain the above men-

mentioned principles in the fame proportions. For laborious and ftrong exercifes, a full age, fever, &c. by encreafing its celerity, augments the proportion of craffamentum, the rednefs, the difpofition to coagulate, and the cohefion of its parts : and the fame means exert a fimilar influence, on the hardnefs, weight, and alkaline principles of the concreted ferum ; on the contrary the younger the animal and the more it is fubjected to a fedentary life, living upon a watery or vegetable diet, the red cruor is proportionately leffened and the quantity of ferum and mucus encreafed. Similar confequences are likewife induced by . *old age.*

Sanguification is effected by a peculiar affimilating action of the veffels on the recently abforbed chyle, which abounds more or lefs in nutritious particles, according to the quantities of gelatinous lymph contained in our aliments.

This chyle when prepared from vegetable food, is always of a thinner confiftence than

than the blood itfelf; having entered the circulation it temperates the putrefcent acrimony; by its diluting quality it prevents the threatened coagulation, and reduces the whole mafs to that medium of faline nature and confiftence which is moft natural to man.

Such chyle as is principally derived from animal food, or farinaceous vegetables, and is replete with the gelatinous lymph, being applied to the vacuities of each broken folid, ferves to repair the confumption or wafte made from the body itfelf by the various actions to which it is expofed.

Few efculent vegetables, contain this animal glue fo effential to fanguification; for it is only after many repeated circulations, that, the fmall portion of jelly, which may be obtained from their farinaceous parts, is converted into the nature of our proper juices. The ufe of vegetables is however extremely neceffary, fince they keep the quan-

tity

tity of the blood from exceeding its due bounds, and prevent its tendency to putrefaction.

Animal food alone contains the nutritious lymph ready prepared for the recruit both of our fluids and folids, and being extracted from the broken fibres, and veffels, by the procefs of digeftion ; paffes with the chyle in great abundance to be mixed with the blood.

By ufing animal food alone or in too great quantity, the hot alkalefcent fcurvy, a fierce and favage temper, a peculiar fætor, and leprofy, with a lixivial folution of all the juices, is induced : thefe are only to be cured by a change of diet, to one in which a vegetable acidity is more efpecially abundant.

From the fame mafs of blood propelled through the fyftem, all the fluids of the human body are generated, which by reafon of their affinity to one another, may be reduced to certain and diftinct

2 L

claffes

claffes : the manner of their fecretion and feparation from the other component parts of the blood,
we have already faid muft be accounted for by the
fabric, mechanifm, and peculiar action of their
refpective fecretory organs, but an explanation of
this would not be effential to our prefent purpofe,
and would confiderably extend the limits of this
effay ; we muft therefore refer to thofe authors
who have wrote exprefsly on the fubject*.

The blood as we have before obferved undergoes a change in paffing through the arteries
into the veins, this has been fuppofed to arife
from the arterial blood having fuffered the action
of the lungs ; this explanation however would
feem to convey fo vague and indeterminate a
meaning, that we cannot help again repeating,
that it moft probably depends on a feparation of
fome portion of its conftituent parts having taken
place previous to its paffing into the venous fyf-

* Vide Hendy, Haller, Monro, and others.

tem ;

tem; and which are again renewed from the atmofphere in the courfe of the fucceeding circulation.

This difference however, though it were not
fo confiderable as we find it to be, would afford
us very confiderable affiftance in diftinguifhing the
venous from the arterial blood in cafes of hæmorrhagy; it may alfo, in fome degree direct us in
blood-letting, for if after blood has been drawn
and coagulated, it appears of a florid red colour
and the craffamentum and ferum are nearly equal
in quantity, we may infer that the perfon enjoys a tolerably good ftate of health; and from a
deviation of thefe proportions we may form a
pretty accurate judgment of the exiftence of difeafe; as, if there are three parts of ferum to one of
the craffamentum, a debilitated ftate is indicated,
in which cafe we ought to be very cautious not to
bleed too profufely, leaft we fhould exhauft the
mafs of all its red globules, as has fometimes been
the cafe, infomuch that it would not ftain linen.

If

If on the other hand, the craffamentum is moft abundant, we may judge the patient is ftronger, and confequently capable of bearing more copious evacuations.

It was an obfervation of Dr. Akenfide's that in the laft mentioned circumftance he would prefcribe bleeding more freely than even under the appearance of the inflammatory buff. When the craffamentum is not firm, but as it were in a ftate of folution, a weak ftate is always indicated.

Mr. Hewfon obferves that in peripneumonies, though the fize appear in confiderable quantities, yet may not the conftitution bear bleeding. .

It is evident from all thefe confiderations, that without a denfe and red blood, health cannot fubfift, and if a morbid diminution of its quantity takes place, the juices ftagnate, and the whole body becomes pale, cold, and weak; and the

cruor

cruor unlefs diluted with a proper portion of a-
queous parts, congeals in the minute veffels,
producing obftruction, inflammation, and all their
dangerous concomitants.

From the different combinations of thefe principles, and a due confideration of the folid fibres
and veffels, a variety of temperaments are derived;
yet we are aware that neither the various habits
nor temperaments of mankind, can originate *folely*
from any peculiarities in the nature of the blood;
nor ought we to attempt the arrangement or defcription of the different temperaments too fyfte-
matically, nor can we comprehend them under
any diftinct number of modifications, their caufes
and effects being various, and the intermediate
diverfities perhaps ad infinitum.

Hence we are made fenfible of the infinite importance of this heterogeneous fluid, and from a
minute investigation of the various purpofes to
which

which its component parts are applied; we are led to infer, that it muſt be the firſt ſource of *life* and *organization*, and as it were the *primordial rudiments of all animated nature.*

F I N I S.

www.ingramcontent.com/pod-product-compliance
Lightning Source LLC
Chambersburg PA
CBHW060559030726
47498CB00005B/1464